"This was left on my door a week ago."

She handed him a primitive doll with long dark yarn for hair and big green eyes. A little knife was stabbed through the heart. Nathan looked up with shock.

"This is a nasty piece of work. Do you have any idea who left it for you or why?"

"Not a clue."

He set the doll on the coffee table and moved closer to her. "It looks like a threat of some kind."

"I know. I asked my friends, but they couldn't figure out who might have left it for me."

"You have to tell me if anything else like this happens."

"Why? What are you going to do about it?" she asked.

"I don't know, but I do know that even though I haven't known you for very long, I care about you."

"I feel the same way about you." A dusting of pink filled Angel's cheeks. "But, of course, we need to keep things strictly business between us."

STALKED THROUGH THE MIST

CARLA CASSIDY

Harlequin
INTRIGUE

Harlequin®
INTRIGUE™

Recycling programs for this product may not exist in your area.

ISBN-13: 978-1-335-45727-1

Stalked Through the Mist

Copyright © 2025 by Carla Bracale

For questions and comments about the quality of this book, please contact us at CustomerService@Harlequin.com.

TM and ® are trademarks of Harlequin Enterprises ULC.

 Harlequin Enterprises ULC
22 Adelaide St. West, 41st Floor
Toronto, Ontario M5H 4E3, Canada
www.Harlequin.com

Printed in U.S.A.

Carla Cassidy is an award-winning, *New York Times* bestselling author who has written over 170 books, including 150 for Harlequin. She has won the Centennial Award from Romance Writers of America. Most recently she won the 2019 Write Touch Readers' Award for her Harlequin Intrigue title *Desperate Strangers*. Carla believes the only thing better than curling up with a good book is sitting down at the computer with a good story to write.

CAST OF CHARACTERS

Angel Marchant—A beautiful fisherwoman who lives in the swamp. However, somebody is threatening her life and she doesn't know who to trust.

Nathan Merrick—A photographer from the city who quickly becomes enchanted with Angel. Is he really in the swamp to take pictures, or does he have nefarious reasons for being there?

Beau Gustave—A gator hunter who is good friends with Angel. Is he truly a friend or a foe who wants her dead?

Mac Singleton—He buys fish from Angel, but does he want more? And what lengths will he go to in order to make her his own?

Louis Mignot—Another gator hunter who is close to Angel. Does he want what's best for her, or does he want her for himself?

Jacque Augustin—A fisherman who is also Angel's friend. Or is he?

Prologue

Colette Broussard ran wildly through the swamp, gasps of pain and terror escaping her. She had to get away. She needed to escape from the madman who had held her captive for three long months. She had to get away from him before he finished killing her and there was no question in her mind that he would eventually kill her.

She ran, despite her dizziness and disorientation. The tree limbs and brush slapped against her and even the soft whisper of the Spanish moss against her bruised and broken body made her want to scream in pain. But she couldn't scream; if she did, then he might hear her and capture her again.

Time had no meaning as she pushed her body to gain as much distance as possible between her and the monster who had kidnapped her.

It was only when she reached the edge of the swamp that she completely collapsed, unable to push herself and her broken body any longer. She fell to her knees and then to the ground where she curled up into a fetal ball.

She closed her eyes, unable to hold them open. As she remained there, she became conscious of her heartbeat.

It was slow and irregular. She was going to die here. The monster had killed her despite her escape from him.

That was her last thought before a wave of darkness called to her and she eagerly sought it to escape her pain.

Chapter One

The sunset glinted on the water and painted the entire swamp in a soft golden light. Birds sang their swan songs for the day from the tops of the cypress and tupelo trees that dripped with Spanish moss.

Angel Marchant used a push pole to guide her pirogue toward the back of her shanty. The fish she'd caught this evening would make a nice gift for her parents. Once she reached her shanty's back deck, she tied up the boat and then grabbed the stringer of fish to carry to her parents' place.

She moved through the swampland with ease, knowing from her twenty-seven years of living here exactly where to step and when to jump over the unexpected pools of water that appeared.

It didn't take her long to be at her parents' shanty. "Hey, Dad," she yelled in greeting as she crossed the wooden bridge that led to the front door of the small home on stilts.

The door opened and her father smiled at her. John Marchant had always been a tall man, but arthritis in his back bent him over slightly at the waist. Still, he was a handsome man with salt-and-pepper hair and dark eyes that gazed at her with obvious love. "Angel, what a pleasant surprise," he said and stepped aside to allow her entry.

Angel's mother, Maria, got up from the chair where she'd been sitting. Maria was still a beautiful woman with long black hair and dark green eyes. "Angel, we didn't expect to see you today," she said and kissed her daughter on the cheek.

Angel was very close to her parents, who had raised her with absolute and unconditional love and taught her love and respect for the swamp.

The shanty was three rooms. The living area and kitchen were small, as was the single bedroom and bathroom. During her years at home, Angel had slept on a cot next to the potbellied stove where her mother cooked all their meals.

"I brought you some fish," Angel said and handed her father the stringer. "There's several good catfish there."

"I see that. Looks like dinner to me, right, Mama?" John said as he carried the fish to the metal bin that served as a sink.

"Right," Maria agreed. "I'll fry them up here in just a few minutes. Thank you, Angel, you want to stay to eat with us?"

"Thanks, but no thanks. I'm actually thinking about getting some of my friends together tonight for a few beers. It's been a while since we've all been together," Angel replied.

"Why don't you sit a spell and visit," John said. "Have you heard about Colette Broussard?"

"No, was her body found?" Angel sank down on the sofa next to her father.

Colette Broussard was one of five people who had just disappeared without a trace from the swamp. Colette had been missing for over three months and most people had just assumed she, along with the others, were dead.

"What I heard in town this morning is that she was found half-naked and unconscious near Fisherman's Tree. She'd been beaten badly and had rope marks around her wrists and ankles," John said.

"That's horrible, but it gives me a little hope for the other people who have been missing," Angel replied. "Hopefully the others are still alive and she'll be able to lead Etienne to where they're all being held." A chill threatened to walk up her spine as she thought of the person who had been dubbed the Swamp Soul Stealer, a monster who made people disappear without a trace.

Etienne Savoie was not only the chief of police for the small town of Crystal Cove, but also for the swamp area that half surrounded the town. He was a good man who had been working hard on the missing persons cases.

"I don't know about that," John replied. "According to Louis at the grocery store, it's not a sure thing that she'll even survive."

"God bless her soul," Maria said as she sat back down in the chair facing the sofa. "I hope you're being very careful, Angel." She looked at her daughter worriedly.

"Don't worry, I'm very careful when I'm out and

about," Angel assured her mother. "Besides, I take little sister with me whenever I leave my house."

"Little sister?" Angel's father looked at her curiously.

Angel pulled out the knife she carried in a sheath on a belt around her waist and beneath her clothes. It was a wickedly sharp fishing knife that could gut a man with a single thrust. She had started wearing it when the second person, a young man in her friend group named Luka Lurance, had gone missing.

"Don't be afraid to use it if need be," her father said.

"Don't worry. I take my own safety very seriously," Angel replied with a small laugh. "And on that note, I think I'll head back home before it gets any later." She stood and her father got up as well. "I'll see you in the next day or two. If you need anything, call me."

A few moments later Angel headed back down the bridge and then took off in the direction of her own shanty. She not only brought her parents fish occasionally, but she also fished for a living, selling what she caught to the local grocery store and the café in town.

As she slowly walked down the narrow trail that would lead her home, she drew in a deep breath of the scents that surrounded her. It was the scents of green things and various flowers and beneath that the faint smell of decay.

She loved living in the swamp. Some of her friends were working hard to save up enough money to leave the marshlands behind forever, but Angel had never wanted to live anyplace else. The swamp was in her blood…in her very soul.

Her thoughts turned to the people she was hoping

to gather this evening for a little social time. Besides Angel, there were three women and three men who had run the swamp as young kids and grown to trust and rely on each other. Their friendship bond was tight and they were definitely ride or die for each other.

She hadn't gone far when she heard it—a deep cry for help coming from someplace off the trail she was on. Each and every muscle in her body tensed as she slowly followed the cries. Was this somehow a ruse? Did a man really need help or was he just pretending to in order to draw somebody close to him?

With the earlier talk about the Swamp Soul Stealer fresh in her head, she pulled the knife sheath out of the top of her jeans where the knife could be grabbed quickly by her if necessary.

She came to another narrow trail and the voice sounded closer. It was definitely a male and distress filled his deep voice. She continued to creep closer and then she saw him. He sat on the edge of the path. His dark hair gleamed in the dappled sunlight that cast through the trees and she could see his lower right leg was bloody.

He looked up at the sound of her approach and his blue eyes gazed at her in obvious relief. A jolt of electricity shot through her. Lordy, but the man was totally hot.

"Hi," he said. "Uh…my name is Nathan Merrick and I seem to have cut my leg pretty badly. Uh…is it possible you could just help me to get back up on my feet? Then I should be able to get to my car and to my motel room in town."

It was obvious this wasn't a ruse. The man's leg was definitely injured and appeared to still be bleeding badly. "I can help you up." She walked close enough to him and then saw he had in his hand a fancy-looking camera case. "Put that down," she instructed and held out both her hands toward him.

He placed the camera case on the side next to him and then reached out and grabbed her hands. Again, an electric tingle flooded through her. His hands were big and warm as they gripped hers.

She yanked on him and he rose to his feet, but instantly groaned as he tried to put pressure on his injured leg. He listed heavily to his good leg as she picked up his camera case and handed it to him.

"Thank you," he said and then took a couple of limping steps forward that made the wound on his leg bleed even more.

"You're welcome, but I think you aren't going to make it all the way to your car and back into town the way that gash is bleeding. My shanty isn't far from here. Come with me and I'll bandage you up and then you can be on your way," she said.

"Really? Thank you so much. I can't tell you how much I would appreciate it." He winced again and she moved to his side so he could lean on her.

It was odd that despite his broad shoulders and solid build, she felt no real fear of him. Maybe it was because a man who groaned under his breath with each step he took didn't seem like much of a threat.

"Who do I send the thank-you flowers to?" he asked as they began to walk.

"What do you mean?" she asked.

"I mean when a lady walks you to her house and offers first-aid services, I should at least know her name," he replied. He gazed at her intently. God, the man had gorgeous eyes with long dark lashes. He smelled yummy, like what she'd always thought a fresh ocean breeze would smell like.

"Oh, I'm Angel… Angel Marchant," she replied.

"You're certainly my angel at the moment," he said with a friendly smile. "I was afraid I was going to be out there bleeding all night long."

"Do you know what you cut yourself on?" she asked.

"I don't have a clue," he replied. "I just took one step and something sharp cut me. I tried to look around to see what it was, but I couldn't find anything."

"That's my place just ahead," she said.

Her shanty lived on stilts like so many others in the swamp. It was larger than her parents' place, although it was also only three rooms. She had spent a lot of her money on the structure itself, making sure it was solidly built for a woman living alone.

She continued to help him across the bridge that led to her porch and then she unlocked her door. Once it was open, she guided him to the sofa and he sank down.

"Let me go get some supplies and I'll be right back," she said. She went into her bathroom, which held a tiny closet with shelves. On one of them was a first-aid kit and also a container with more injury supplies. She added in several wet washcloths and a tub full of water to clean up the blood.

Before she carried it out, she took a few moments

to draw in several deep breaths. Finding an injured stranger was certainly not a common thing. Finding an injured totally hot man in the swamp had definitely never happened to her before.

As attractive as he was, she knew nothing about him and in any case, she just intended to bandage up his leg and then send him on his way. She needed to get to it before complete darkness fell.

He had the look of the city all over him, from the scent of his cologne to the make of the khaki shorts and the khaki-and-dark-green-patterned short-sleeved button-up shirt he wore. He didn't look like a man who would be comfortable finding his way out of the swamp in the dark.

With that thought in mind, she left the bathroom and returned to where he remained sitting on the sofa with his leg propped up on the coffee table.

"I normally don't put my feet up on the furniture, but I didn't want to bleed all over your sofa or the pretty rug on the floor," he said.

"Thank you for being thoughtful about that." She set her items on the coffee table next to his leg and then she sat on the table so she could minister to him. "I'm sorry, but I'm probably going to hurt you."

"I understand," he replied.

She felt his gaze on her as she began to wipe away the excess blood. Thankfully at some point the big gash had finally stopped bleeding. But it still oozed and it was definitely a nasty wound.

He only tensed up once and that was when she poured alcohol on the gash to clean it out. "If you don't mind my asking, what were you doing out in the swamp. You don't look like you belong here," she said as she began to bandage up the wound.

"Actually, I'm a biologist and I've been studying and photographing the flora and fauna here in the swamp. I've been commissioned to write a book about swamps. Unfortunately, I barely got started before this happened."

She looked up at him in surprise. A biologist? She'd never met anyone like him before. He smiled at her. "In other words, I'm a nerd…a science nerd."

She quickly looked back down at his leg. He certainly didn't look like a nerd. He was way too hot to be a nerd. "I think that will do it," she said as she finished wrapping the last of the bandage around his leg. "If I were you, I'd see a doctor in town first thing tomorrow."

"I will, and I can't thank you enough for everything you've done for me," he said.

"I couldn't very well walk away from you and let you bleed to death," she replied.

"Well, I'll just get out of your hair now." He went to stand up and instantly fell back on the sofa. He tried to stand again but it was obvious his leg was still weak and hurt too much to hold his weight.

She looked out the window where darkness had completely fallen. It was at least a fifteen-minute walk to get out of the swamp to where he'd probably parked his car. How could she just put him out in the dark when he could barely walk?

"It's obvious your leg is still hurting you badly," she said. "You can spend the night here on my sofa and hopefully you'll be well enough to walk out of here tomorrow."

He frowned, the gesture doing nothing to detract from his handsome features. "Are you sure that would be okay?"

"Positive," she replied. "I'll just go get you a pillow and a sheet to help you get comfortable."

She went into her bedroom and closed the door behind her. It was odd, but she felt no fear of him. Still, he was a stranger and she really knew nothing about him, and she was a woman all alone.

With these thoughts in mind, she pulled her cell phone out of her back pocket and quickly called one of her best friends, Shelby Santori. "Shelby, I need a big favor from you."

"What do you need?" Shelby asked.

"Can you spend the night here tonight? I know it's late notice, but I would really appreciate it."

"Sure…but why?"

"I discovered a man in the swamp. He has an injured leg and so I told him he could sleep on my sofa for tonight. But I'd feel far more comfortable if somebody else was here with me."

"I'll be there in fifteen or so," Shelby said without asking any more questions.

Angel gathered up the sleeping items for Nathan and then carried them back into the living room and set them all down on the chair that faced her sofa. She lit several lanterns in the room and then sank down on the sofa in the opposite corner from him.

"I can't believe you're going to so much trouble for me," he said.

"You needed help. Folks here in the swamp don't walk away from people who need help," she replied. "How does your leg feel now?"

"I could try to be a macho man and tell you it's feeling just fine, but the truth of the matter is it hurts like hell."

"I'm sorry I don't have anything to give you to help with the pain," she replied.

"That's okay. It should start feeling better with each hour that passes."

Once again, she could smell the totally awesome scent of him and his body heat warmed her in a distinctly pleasant way. Lordy, but she found the man attractive.

However, he was simply a stranger that was spending the night and would be gone tomorrow.

Angel was the most beautiful woman Nathan had seen in years. Her black hair cascaded down her back in a curtain of richness. Her eyes were an interesting shade of green and rimmed with long dark lashes. Her features were delicate and amazingly attractive. However her mouth was wide and generous and her lips were plump and lush, only adding to her overall beauty.

She was clad in a pair of jeans that showcased her long legs and a fitted navy T-shirt that emphasized her slender waist and medium-sized breasts. God, but she was gorgeous.

"You have a nice place here," he said.

"Thank you, I love it here."

The room felt cozy with the sofa and chair and also a small potbellied stove. There was a small bookcase that held not only books, but also some knickknacks.

The kitchen area held a small table with four chairs and a sink and countertop. That was all he could see from his vantage point. The floors were a rich wood and covered by several braided rugs in vivid colors.

"You were born in the swamp?" he asked. He was interested in everything about her.

She nodded. "Not too far from here. I was born in the swamp as were my parents and my grandparents and so on," she replied.

"If you don't mind my asking, what do you do for a living out here?" He had no idea if he was getting too personal or not, but he was definitely curious about her and her life here.

"I fish for a living," she replied. "I sell the fish I catch to the grocery store and café in town." At that moment there was a knock on her door. "Excuse me," she said. "My friend and I had planned a sleepover for tonight and I haven't had a chance to call her to cancel."

"Please don't cancel your plans on my account. I'll just sit here and be quiet and try to disappear into the furniture," he replied.

She got up and went to the door. A woman swept in and stopped at the sight of him. She appeared to be about Angel's age and, while pretty, she didn't hold a candle to Angel. She carried with her a small overnight bag.

"Well, what a surprise," she said. "Hi, I'm Shelby Santori."

"I'm Nathan Merrick, and Angel rescued me when I cut my leg." He gestured toward his bandaged leg.

"That's our Angel, always ready to help anyone who needs it," Shelby replied. She looked at Angel. "So, are we still on for tonight?"

"Please, whatever the two of you had planned, don't cancel because of me," Nathan said.

"All we had planned was getting into Angel's bed and gossiping for half the night," Shelby replied with a laugh.

"Uh…before we do that, could I get you something to eat?" Angel asked him as she moved the pillow and sheet from the chair to one end of the sofa.

Despite the fact that it was getting late, Nathan had no appetite. Besides, out here in the swamp he doubted she could just whip something up for him without a lot of trouble and the last thing he wanted to do was cause her any more trouble.

"No, thanks. I'm really not hungry, although I wouldn't mind some water," he replied.

"Of course," she replied. She walked over to the kitchen area and pulled a bottle of water from what appeared to be a built-in small refrigerator. She walked back over and handed it to him. "I'll leave the lamps burning for you and the bathroom is the doorway on the left. Is there anything else I can do for you?"

"No, you've done far more than enough. I'll never be able to thank you enough for your kindness," he replied. "I'll be fine here for tonight."

"Great," Shelby said and grabbed Angel by the arm.

"Come on, girlfriend. We have a lot to talk about to-night."

"Good night, Nathan. I hope you sleep well," Angel said and then Shelby pulled her into a room he assumed was Angel's bedroom. The door closed behind them and then there was silence.

Except there wasn't complete silence as he became aware of bullfrogs croaking and water gently lapping against the stilts that held the shanty up.

He settled into the sofa with his head on the pillow and the sheet covering him. The pillow smelled like the woman… He'd noticed Angel's beguiling fragrance when she was supporting him on the walk to this place. It was the scent of mysterious flowers and spices…very alluring.

He was ridiculously drawn to her, but tomorrow he'd be leaving here and he doubted he'd ever see her again. His leg hurt badly, but with the rhythm of the frogs croaking and the water lapping, he fell asleep and into pleasant dreams about Angel.

Chapter Two

Nathan awakened around dawn. His leg still ached, but he managed to make it to the bathroom and then back to the sofa. He hadn't been sitting there too long when the bedroom door opened and Angel and Shelby came into the living room. Angel wore a pair of denim shorts and a red T-shirt and once again looked positively stunning.

"Good morning," both the women said to him at the same time.

"Good morning to you two," he replied.

"How is your leg feeling this morning?" Angel asked.

"It still hurts, but not quite as badly. I should be able to get out of your house this morning," he said.

"Let me make you some breakfast before you go," Angel said.

"And that's my cue to get out of here," Shelby said. "It was nice meeting you, Nathan. And girlfriend, I'll talk to you later." With that, Shelby left.

"I'm just going to go start up my generator, I'll be right back." Angel disappeared out a back door in the kitchen. He heard a faint thrum and then she came back in.

"So, you have a generator to give you electricity when you want it?" he asked.

"Yes, I use it to charge my phone and I have a two-burner electric cooktop for when I don't want to make a fire and cook on the potbellied stove," she explained.

She remained in the kitchen area. "I hope you like eggs and toast because that's what's on the menu this morning."

"That sounds great, but you really don't have to cook for me. You've already done more than enough."

"It's a rule of mine," she said and offered him a bright smile. "I never send a wounded man back out to the swamp without fixing him eggs and toast."

He returned her smile. "Far be it from me to be the man who makes you break your rule." From his vantage point, he couldn't really see what she was doing. "Do you mind if I come and sit at your table?"

"Not at all, in fact, I'm making a pot of coffee right now."

He was definitely looking forward to a cup of coffee, but even though he intended to leave here, she still intrigued him. Her lifestyle was so different from his. She was so different from any other woman he had ever known before.

He moved to the table and watched as she got a four-cup coffee maker out, plugged it into an outlet on the wall and then got it working. She then pulled out the two-burner stovetop and set it on the counter.

"Do you have a cell phone you want me to plug in?" she asked as she plugged in her own.

"I have a cell phone, but I don't have the charger with

me and in any case, I can do that once I get back to the motel." He watched as she then pulled an iron skillet out of a lower cabinet.

"And now, for the most important question of the day…" she said and turned to look at him. "How do you like your eggs?"

"Any way you want to make them," he replied. The scent of fresh coffee filled the room and she poured him a cup and set it before him.

"Ah, thank you…the nectar of the gods," he said.

She laughed, the sound musical and very pleasant. "So, you're one of those," she said and raised one of her perfect dark eyebrows.

He laughed. "One of what?"

"One who likes to be fueled by caffeine."

He laughed again. "Actually, I'm a two-cup man in the morning and that's it. I much prefer sports drinks for the rest of the day."

"Well, I hope you like cheesy scrambled eggs because that's what I'm making."

"How did you know that that's my favorite breakfast?" he replied lightly.

She turned to look at him again. "Are you always so pleasant?"

"I try to be," he said more seriously. "I spend so much of my work time by myself either in my lab or in a field or a marsh that when I'm around people, I always try to be friendly and respectful."

"That's a nice way to be," she replied.

She grabbed a small container of milk, a bag of

shredded cheese and a carton of eggs from the mini built-in refrigerator that blended in with her cabinets.

"How do you manage to keep your refrigerator running? I know you just turned on your generator a little while ago," he asked.

"Oh, it's not a refrigerator, it's a cooler. About three times a week I go into town and buy blocks of ice for it." She pulled a toaster out of the cabinet and set it on the counter.

"Sorry I have so many questions, but I've never been in one of the shanties before and I find it all very interesting. In fact, yesterday was the first time I'd actually been in a swamp. I've studied them extensively by sitting at my desk, but I'd never actually been in one."

This time the look she gave him held a little bit of suspicion. "Then how on earth did you get commissioned for a book about swamps?"

A small laugh escaped him. "I wrote a proposal filled with my credentials and all the things I intended to deliver and much to my surprise, they offered me a contract. So, here I am."

She mixed together the eggs, milk and cheese and then poured it all into the awaiting skillet. She got out a loaf of bread and put four slices in the toaster. Finally, she pulled from the cooler a small container of soft butter.

"Why Crystal Cove?" she asked. "Out of all the swamps in the world, why here?"

"First of all, I live in New Orleans, so this was only five or so hours away. The second reason is I fell in love with the name, Crystal Cove. It just sounded so pleasant. The little town is big enough to have a decent motel, but small enough to have real character."

"The nice thing about it is for the most part the townspeople and swamp people get along and respect each other," she replied.

"That's a good thing. From what I've learned, it's not that way everywhere," he replied.

As she finished up the meal, he fell silent and just watched her. She moved with efficiency and grace. If he wasn't careful, he could become quite smitten with her.

It took only a few minutes and then the plates were on the table and she sat across from him. "Enjoy," she said.

"Thank you." He took a sip of the coffee. It was just the way he liked it…strong and black.

"There is one thing you need to be aware of as you go out and about in the swamp," she said.

"And what's that?"

Her eyes appeared to darken. "You need to have a weapon with you whenever you travel. There's somebody out there who is kidnapping people from the swamp and we don't know whether they have been murdered or are being held somewhere."

"Oh, yeah, I read a little bit about it in the paper. He's called the soul sucker or something like that?" He hadn't paid too much attention to the small story on the second page of the *Crystal Cove News*.

"The Swamp Soul Stealer has taken two men and three women. However, one woman who has been missing for three months turned up yesterday half dead from being beaten and bound. This monster is somebody everyone in the swamp should fear."

"What kind of weapon do you carry?" he asked.

"A fishing knife that could gut a man with a single thrust."

"And you could do that?"

"If it was to defend my life, damn right I could do that," she replied firmly. "Now, eat your eggs before they get cold."

He imagined she had to be an incredibly strong woman to live out here all alone. There weren't many conveniences in the swamp, so life out here had to be far more difficult than living in a city or town.

They ate for a few minutes in silence and then began to small-talk about the hot weather and the swamp. "I'll bet you know most of the plants here," he said.

She smiled and once again he was struck by her beauty. "I certainly don't know their fancy scientific names, but yes, I can identify a lot of the plants. My parents were very good teachers when it came to the plant and animal life here in the swamp."

"You said you fish for a living. How does that work?"

"I have some baited lines in the water that I check every morning and sometimes I sit on the bank and fish from there. I have a cage floating off my back porch where I put the fish until I have enough gathered up to make a trip into town," she explained.

"And you can make enough money doing that to survive?" he asked and immediately said, "I'm sorry, I might have gotten too personal."

"No, not at all. I make enough money to fill my basic

needs. All I really require is ice for my cooler, gas for my generator and money for my cell phone bill. And at the end of the year, I pay some taxes on this place. I'm saving any extra money I get for some more updates to the shanty."

"And you love living here," he said.

"How do you know that?" She raised one eyebrow again.

"Because your eyes light up when you talk about the swamp and you become quite animated," he replied.

She laughed. "You read me right. And I'll bet I can read you fairly well, too."

"Go for it."

"You love what you do because your face lights up when you talk about your flora and fauna," she said, making him laugh. "But I can't read you about your personal life because you haven't told me anything about it. Are you married? Do you have children?"

"I'm single with no significant other and I have no children. I live in a house but rarely spend much time there. I teach classes at a small community college and if I'm not in the classroom, I'm in the lab or in the field."

"Out of all the flora and fauna in the world, why swamps?" She got up and carried their now-empty plates to the sink, and returned with the coffeepot.

"I've always been curious about swamps," he said. "Thanks," he added as she topped off his coffee. "Growing up in New Orleans, the marshes were part of the landscape. Did you know that swamps have a near perfect ecosystem? It's amazing how the plants all work together to support this system." He realized he was talking too much. "Sorry, I was about to go off on a tangent."

"It's okay, don't apologize for being passionate about your work," she replied.

He was really quite taken with her attractiveness. Her long dark hair begged him to run his fingers through it at the same time her lush lips looked ready for a wild, hot kiss.

Damn, what was wrong with him? It didn't matter how beautiful she was or how easy he found it to talk to her. It didn't matter that she was unique and intrigued him.

In minutes, he was going to walk out of here and would never see her again unless… "Angel, would you be interested in working for me as a guide of sorts. I'll pay you daily." He mentioned a figure that he knew was a bit generous.

Her eyes widened slightly. "Are you serious?"

"Very serious. I'm sure you know this swamp very well and I don't know it at all. I could definitely use someone to help me get around. All you'd have to do is guide me while I take photographs. So, are you interested?"

"Uh… I don't know. I'd have to think about it."

He finished his coffee. "How long would you need to think about it?"

"I could have an answer for you tomorrow morning," she replied after a moment of hesitation.

"And how would I find you tomorrow morning?" he asked. He had no idea where this shanty was located.

"I'm assuming you parked your car in the lot in front

of the swamp's main path in," she said. "It's a fairly big parking area that's used by most of the people who live here."

"Yes, that sounds right," he replied.

"Then I'll meet you there in the morning and I'll give you my answer," she replied.

"On that note, I've taken up enough of your time." He stood.

She also got up from the table. "I'll walk you out to your car."

He started to protest, but the truth was he needed her help to get back. He'd been in so much pain the day before when she'd helped him get here the last thing he'd been paying attention to was the paths they had taken. "Thank you, I'd really appreciate it."

He limped over to the coffee table and picked up his camera while she grabbed a key and her cell phone. Together they stepped out into the morning light.

The swamp was alive with birds singing from the tops of the trees and the sound of splashing coming from the water. The brush rustled with small animals scurrying about and insects whirred their own little songs.

"Sorry, I can't move too fast," he said as he followed her down the bridge and onto the trail.

"That's okay." She flashed him a smile over her shoulder. "I never mind a leisurely walk through the swamp."

She was virtually a stranger, albeit a very kind one, but that didn't explain the way her smile warmed him. He followed behind her and she did walk slow enough for him to keep up. His leg still hurt quite a bit, but not nearly as bad as it had the day before.

They didn't talk as they made their way through the jungle-like maze. It seemed to take forever, but finally they broke into the clearing where his car was parked.

"Angel, I know I've said this before, but I can't thank you enough for your kindness in helping me out," he said as she turned to look at him.

"You were a very easy houseguest," she replied.

"And about the job offer. I really hope you'll consider it."

"Why don't we do this. If I'm in, I'll meet you here tomorrow morning at seven thirty. If I'm not in, I won't be here. It was nice meeting you, Nathan." With that, she turned around and disappeared back into the tangled greenery of the swamp.

Nathan got into his car, but didn't start it up right away. Instead he sat and thought about the woman who had just left him.

There was no question she was gorgeous, but aside from that, something nebulous drew him toward her. He wanted more of her. He wanted to know her better and he hadn't felt this kind of interest in a woman in a very long time.

He finally started his engine and pulled out of the parking lot. All he could hope for was that she'd be there in the morning.

The next morning around six Angel sat on the bank at her favorite fishing spot. But instead of thinking about catching fish, her thoughts were consumed with thoughts of Nathan Merrick.

There was no question she'd found him extremely attractive. It had been a long time since she'd been interested in a man.

Her last relationship had been four years ago. Jim Fortiner had been a townie and they had dated for a little over two years. She'd thought Jim was her forever man until she'd found out on the nights he wasn't with her, he was with another woman. His double life and utter betrayal had broken her and it had taken her a long time to finally get over it.

Now, at twenty-seven years old, she considered herself older and wiser and just because Nathan was a good-looking, seemingly nice guy, didn't mean she wanted anything more to do with him…or did she?

She'd gone back and forth in her head all night long about the offer to be his guide. When she'd talked to Shelby about it the day before, Shelby thought she'd be crazy not to do it.

"You could build that new deck you've been talking about or buy a bigger, better generator with the kind of money he's offering you. Seriously, Angel, why on earth wouldn't you do it?" Shelby had said. "It's perfect for you."

Why not, indeed. Maybe she was hesitant because she'd felt an unexpected spark with him, an attraction that she hadn't felt in a very long time. She had a feeling spending more time with him would only draw her closer to him and what was the point of that?

He lived in New Orleans, a four-and-a-half-hour

drive from here. He was a scientist who was highly educated. She'd been homeschooled by her mother. They couldn't be more different from each other. Of course he hadn't said anything to indicate to her that he had any interest in her other than her knowledge of the swamp.

And it was far too soon for her to know if she liked him or not. He may be a jerk at heart. Just because he'd been pleasant to her for a night and a morning, didn't mean she would find him pleasant if she knew him better.

At seven o'clock she packed up her fishing supplies and headed home. She left the items on her back deck and then headed toward the parking area.

She hadn't even realized she'd made up her mind to take him up on the offer until she was on her way. She had no idea how long he might want to use her as a guide, but there was no question the money he had offered her could be put to good use.

It didn't take her long to get to the parking area. He was already there standing outside his car. "Angel," he said with a big smile that warmed her more than the morning sun. "You came."

She couldn't help but return his smile. He looked so handsome clad in a royal blue polo that matched the color of his eyes and emphasized his broad shoulders. He also had on a pair of dark blue shorts with a fresh bandage on his calf.

"You offered me a job with pay that I couldn't resist so I decided to come," she replied. Ultimately that's why she was here. Not because Nathan was superhot or that she was somehow drawn to him. This was strictly a business relationship and nothing more.

"So, the first thing we need to hash out is how you want to be paid. I'm assuming you want cash. Do you want to be paid daily? Weekly?"

"Daily," she replied. The *weekly* had thrown her off a little bit. "Uh, how long do you expect this all to take?"

"To be honest, I don't have a real answer. It will take as long as it takes…until I have all the photos I feel like I need to complete the book."

"Do you want to get started today?" she asked.

"Sure, that would be great," he agreed.

"Then let's get started," she replied. She watched as he opened his car door and retrieved his camera. He took the cap off the lens and then nodded.

"How's your leg this morning?" she asked as they entered into the swamp on the path.

"Still hurting, but a bit better," he replied.

"Where exactly would you like to go or what would you like to focus on for the day?" She paused and turned to face him. He stood close enough to her that she could smell the scent of shaving cream mingling with his attractive, slightly spicy and fresh cologne.

"Maybe today we could focus on some of the animals who live here," he said. "Would that be possible?"

"Sure, we can do that," she replied. "I know where the gators lurk and the turtles snap. I also know where the wild boars stay. Keep your camera handy because there are a lot of animals here."

"Just give me a minute. I think I need to change my lens." She watched with interest as he took off the one

that had been on the camera and replaced it with a longer one. He grinned at her. "This way I can take photos
from far away so a gator doesn't get a chance to eat me."

When he grinned like that, it gave him a new attractiveness that created a warmth deep in the pit of
her stomach. "I also added a stun gun to my collection
of toys this morning so that soul sucker fellow won't
get me."

She laughed. "That helps, but I think we're safe in
numbers and during the daylight. In any case, you can
stun him and then I'll gut him."

"We're definitely a dangerous duo, so bad guys be-
ware," he replied. For a moment their eye contact held.
Oh, she could fall into the depths of his beautiful blue
eyes.

She quickly turned around. "Follow me," she said.
"I'll take you to some of the gators first."

They walked in silence. She didn't want to get to
know him better because she was afraid she might like
him too much. *Strictly business*, she reminded herself.

Tonight she planned to be with the people she belonged with…her fellow swamp friends. She certainly
didn't belong with somebody like Nathan. She realized
she was probably overthinking things. He hadn't shown
her any indication he felt the same attraction toward her
that she felt toward him.

"You doing okay?" she asked as the path narrowed
and they walked deeper into the swamp.

"I'm fine," he replied.

She could move pretty soundlessly through the
swamp, but there was no way they were going to sneak

up on anything with him making so much noise as he followed behind her. She could tell he was heavily favoring his good leg.

There was a part of her that admired his determination to do his job despite the injury that still had to hurt badly. "Are you under some sort of a deadline?" she asked.

"Not a real firm deadline, but I'd like to have the photos taken in the next month or so," he replied.

A month, and then he'd be gone. All the more reason to keep things strictly professional between them, she told herself. She continued to lead him toward the deep pool of water that several big gators called home.

"We talked about my personal life, but I don't know much about yours. Do you have a significant other?" he asked.

"No, there's nobody special in my life right now," she replied.

"Your friend Shelby seemed very nice," he said.

"She's the best. We've been friends since we were about six. Our parents were friends. She's only one of my friends here in the swamp. In fact, I'm planning on getting them all together tonight for drinks. If you'd like to come, you're more than welcome. It will probably be around seven." What was she doing inviting him to spend time with her after hours?

"Thanks for the invite," he replied. "I'd love to meet your friends."

"We can talk about it more later," she replied, vaguely surprised by his answer. Of course he was a stranger in town. Maybe he just needed a little social time. That certainly didn't explain why she had invited him in the first place.

By that time they had reached a small cove. Cypress and tupelo trees with their complicated root structures rose up out of the water and dripped with Spanish moss.

There was a quiet, almost mysterious hush here and a pristine, primitive beauty. Nathan stepped up next to her and began to snap photos of the trees. His camera clicked and whirred over and over again.

The sound drew the gators from their resting places. Dark eyes and snouts appeared in the water, obviously curious about this new noise.

Nathan continued to snap photos, quietly gasping as one of the kings of the swamp showed his entire massive body. He took a step closer and his foot slipped, sending him into the water. He gasped, yet managed to hold his camera up over his head and Angel quickly leaned over and grabbed it from him.

She set it on the ground. The loud splash of him falling into the water had called the gators even closer. As he tried to climb back up onto the bank, he slipped down once again. A slight panic lit his eyes and it wasn't until Angel grabbed his hand that he managed to get up out of the water and back on shore.

He rose up directly in front of her, so close she could feel his breath on her face and see the tiny shards of silver in the irises of his eyes.

For a moment she was breathless and her body didn't get her brain's command to step back from him. He remained unmoving as well. His eyes sparked with something that looked like desire and that made her feet move backward and away from him.

"Thanks for helping me out," he finally said, further breaking the awkward moment. "I almost became that big guy's breakfast."

"I should have warned you how slick the bank's edge was," she said.

"Well again, thanks for hauling me out of there."

"No problem. I'm not a big fan of watching gators eat photographers."

He laughed. "Thank God. I'm not a big fan of getting eaten by a gator." He bent over and picked up his camera. "Thank goodness this stayed dry, but since I'm soaking wet, I think this is going to be a very short day. Of course I'll certainly pay you for a full day."

"I'm not worried about that. If fact, since this was such a short day, you don't have to pay me at all."

"We'll see about that," he replied.

She led him back to where his car was parked. Despite his clothes being soaked, he stopped along the way to take more pictures of the plants they passed.

They were silent on the walk back to his car. When they finally reached it, he opened the car door and put his camera inside and then turned to face her. He began to pull his wallet out of his wet pants, but she waved her hands to stop him.

"Really, you don't owe me anything for today," she said emphatically.

"Are you sure? I took up much of your morning."

She smiled. "I've had worse things take up my mornings."

"Is the invite still good for tonight?" he asked.

"Definitely," she replied. "Maybe we should exchange cell phone numbers just in case things don't work out with my friends tonight."

"We should probably do that anyway since we're working together," he agreed. "Hang on, my cell phone is in my glove box." He slid into the driver's seat, retrieved the phone and then got back out of the car.

It took them only moments to exchange numbers. "If we're on for tonight, I'll just meet you here around six," she said. "And if things don't work out for tonight, I'll give you a call."

"Sounds good to me." He smiled at her and once again an inexplicable warmth swept through her. "Then hopefully I'll see you later this evening."

She stepped back from his car and watched as he pulled out of the parking lot. It was only when his car disappeared from sight that she turned and headed back to her shanty.

She wasn't sure exactly what to make of Nathan Merrick. She especially wasn't sure what to make of her crazy attraction to him. There had been that moment when she'd helped him out of the water that she irrationally thought he might kiss her. What was even more irrational was that she might have welcomed it.

The only thing she did know for sure was she couldn't wait for the evening to come.

Chapter Three

Nathan was thrilled not to get a call canceling the evening plans. He was looking forward to seeing Angel with her friends. The morning with her had been rather awkward. He'd been self-conscious and the unexpected dip in the swamp hadn't helped matters any. He'd been embarrassed by his own clumsiness and needing her to rescue him by pulling him out of the water.

It had been years since he'd had any kind of a relationship or been on a date. He certainly wasn't looking for anything like that with Angel. He only knew he found her vastly attractive and he wanted to get to know her better. Hopefully this evening he would get that opportunity.

When he'd gotten back to the motel room, he'd changed out of his wet clothes and had also changed his bandage. He'd found a walk-in clinic located in the pharmacy and had had his leg checked out by the nurse on duty.

She had given him a tetanus shot and a tube of antibiotic cream to keep on it. She told him he'd probably needed stitches but since the wound was already closed up and healing, he'd been good to go. At about four o'clock he left his motel again and drove through a burger place called The Big D. He took his burger and fries back to his room and ate.

He showered and shaved and changed the bandage on his leg once again and then dressed in a pair of jeans and another blue polo shirt. He added a couple sprays of his favorite cologne. A glance at the clock told him it was almost time to leave and meet Angel for the evening.

Minutes later, when he got into his car, he was surprised to feel a flutter of nerves rush through his veins. It was the anxiety of meeting new people…people who were very different from him. And truth be told, he wanted to impress Angel, and for her friends to like him.

There had been a minute after she'd pulled him out of the water when they'd stood so close together that he could feel her body heat radiating toward him. He could smell the wonderful scent of her and saw a slight flare in the depths of her green eyes.

In that moment he'd wanted to kiss her. He'd wanted to wrap his arms around her, pull her tight against him and explore those lush, inviting lips of hers. Of course he hadn't done that, but it surprised him that he'd even wanted to.

He was about fifteen minutes early arriving at the parking lot. He sat in his car and stared at the swamp ahead of him. It looked primeval and mysteriously beautiful, like the woman it had spawned.

Even though it had been a short morning, he had snapped dozens of good photos today, capturing a number of plants indigenous to the swamp. He'd also gotten several of the alligators. All in all, it had been a good start to his mission.

At that moment Angel appeared in the clearing. Clad in a pair of black jeans and a dark green tank top, and with her dark hair loose around her shoulders, she looked like part of the surroundings. She appeared as mysteriously beautiful and a bit wild, like the mystifying swamp she came from.

He got out of his car and when she smiled at him, he felt a ridiculous amount of warmth explode in the pit of his stomach. Did her beautiful smile affect all men that way or was it just him?

"Hello, Nathan," she greeted him.

"Hi, Angel."

"Glad you could make it this evening," she said.

"I appreciate the invite. The motel room can get fairly lonely at times."

"Well, you won't be lonely tonight. I've got six of my good friends coming over."

"Sounds like fun to me," he replied.

"Then just follow me and I'll take you to my place." She turned and headed up the path. He followed closely behind her, paying careful attention to the directions as they walked.

"How was the rest of your day today?" he asked.

"Good, how was yours?"

"Once I cleaned the swamp water and embarrassment of my own clumsiness off me, it was fine," he replied.

She laughed and flashed a quick glance back at him. "You had no reason to feel embarrassed. I really should have warned you that the bank was slippery."

From the main path they took a smaller trail to the left and followed that until they came to another fork and she took another left. They didn't go far before her shanty came into view.

He hadn't noticed much about it when she'd brought him here with his injured leg. It looked like an enchanted cabin rising up from the glistening water that surrounded it. It was finished in a dark brown wood but had a cheerful yellow trim around the windows and doorway. He already knew the inside was cozy and surprisingly nice.

They crossed the bridge that led to her porch and then she unlocked her door and ushered him inside.

"Make yourself at home," she said. "The others should trickle in here in the next few minutes. In the meantime beer is on the menu for tonight when it comes to alcoholic drinks. Would you like one?"

"Are you having one?" he asked as he eased down onto one corner of the sofa.

"I am," she replied. She went into the kitchen area, opened her cooler and pulled out two beers. She handed him one and then sat in the chair facing the sofa.

They unscrewed the tops of the bottles at the same time and then she held hers up. "Cheers," she said.

He raised his bottle toward her. "Cheers back at you." He took a drink and then set the bottle on a coaster on the coffee table. "So, you want to tell me about the people I'll be meeting here tonight?"

She took a drink of her beer and then set it on the little end table next to the chair. "You already know

Shelby and she'll be here. Then there's Rosemary Fantiour, she's twenty-three and the baby of the group."

A knock fell on the door. It opened and a tall, physically fit man walked in. He had bold features with high
cheekbones. His long dark hair was tied at the nape of
his neck with a piece of rawhide and he was clad in a
pair of jeans and a navy T-shirt.

Nathan immediately got to his feet and held out a
hand to him. "Nathan Merrick," he said.

The man grabbed his hand in a firm shake. "Louis
Mignot."

Within minutes everyone had arrived. Along with
Shelby, there was Rosemary Fantiour and Marianne La-
Croix to round out the women and Beau Gustave and
Jacques Augustin to round out the men.

All the men were dark-haired, dark-eyed and in great
physical shape. The women were also dark-haired and
pretty, although none of them held a candle to Angel.

Nathan offered his place on the sofa to the women,
but they all declined. Instead kitchen chairs were pulled
in and a couple of the men sprawled on the floor.

Angel brought them all beers and then she settled
back in the chair that had remained vacant. Initially
the talk was of swamp matters…what fish was biting
where and where a new sounder of boars was located.
There was a lot of teasing among the group and it was
obvious they all cared deeply about each other.

Nathan remained quiet, listening and observing
the group dynamics. It was obvious they all respected
Angel and he suspected most of the men might have a
crush on her. And why wouldn't they?

She wasn't just beautiful, but with her friends she was also witty and fun. Nathan enjoyed seeing her this way, relaxed and having a good time. She put out a platter of cheese and crackers and they all began to graze on the offering, and then she lit kerosene lanterns against the encroaching darkness. The lanterns' light created a warm glow in the room.

It wasn't long before the conversation turned to him. "So, I hear you offered Angel some kind of a job," Louis said, his dark eyes sharp and filled with more than a touch of suspicion.

"Yes, I have. It didn't take me long to realize I needed somebody who knows the swamp well to guide me around, so I offered that job to Angel and she accepted."

"And you're getting pictures for a book?" Rosemary asked. She struck a pose. "You can take pictures of me for a book anytime. You can title them fiercest animal in the swamp."

Everyone laughed, including Nathan. The young woman looked about as fierce as a caterpillar. "Tell us exactly what the book is about," Jacques said.

Nathan spent the next few minutes explaining he was a biologist and had scored a book deal based on his studies of plant and animal life in the swamp.

"I've studied swamp life extensively from my desk but had never actually been in a swamp," he explained. "So, I'm here to see things up close and personal and take photos to go along with my writings."

They asked him more questions about where he lived and how long he intended to be there. "I'm planning on being here about a month or so," he replied to that question. "It should take me about that long to get all the photos I need."

"And you're planning on tying up Angel's time for that long?" Beau asked. "You might not realize this, but she has other responsibilities here. She takes care of her parents by bringing them fish and the supplies they might need."

"Beau, I can take care of myself," Angel said.

"I just don't want to see you overdoing things," Beau replied. There was a softness in the man's eyes when he gazed at Angel. Nathan didn't know if Angel knew it or not, but Nathan believed Beau just might be in love with her.

The evening was pleasant, although Beau and Louis continued to eye him with more than a bit of suspicion. Nathan really couldn't blame them. He was a virtual stranger to them and they were just looking out for Angel's welfare.

He learned that Marianne worked as a waitress at the local café. Rosemary had an online business selling potions and notions from the swamp and Shelby worked as a clerk in one of the shops. Louis, along with Beau caught gators for a living and Jacques was also a fisherman. Nathan found them all to be utterly fascinating.

At about ten thirty everyone began to leave. "Nathan, I'm sure we'll be seeing a lot of you," Shelby said to him.

"I hope so. I really enjoyed meeting you all this evening," he replied.

"Yeah, it was nice for you to meet the gang. We bark at each other, but we never bite," Rosemary said.

Nathan laughed. "It reminded me of some of my friends back home."

Within ten more minutes everyone was gone. Nathan carried what was left of the cheese and crackers into the kitchen and set the platter on the countertop while Angel picked up random empty beer bottles left around the room.

"I love my friends, but they're all pigs when it comes to picking up after themselves," Angel said.

Nathan laughed once again. "I get it. I have the same kinds of friends."

She began to put the cheese back into the cooler. "Do you hang out with a bunch of other scientist types?" she asked.

"Actually, I do. I have two good friends who are both biologists and we hang out together when we can. One is married, one is divorced and then there's me."

"It's nice to have good friends," she replied. "By the way, did you get your leg checked out by a doctor today?"

"I used the walk-in clinic at the pharmacy. I got a tetanus shot and she told me I might have needed stitches, but you did such a great job of wrapping it that it would heal nicely without them."

"Oh, that's good news. Now, are you ready to head back to your car?"

"Whenever you're ready." He was still a bit uneasy about finding the parking lot in the dark.

"Then let's take off." As they left her cabin, she locked the door. Today he'd noticed she not only had a regular lock on her front door, but she also had a hasp lock for extra security when she was inside the shanty. Definitely smart for a woman who lived all alone.

He was grateful she'd grabbed a flashlight on the way out. He was relatively sure she didn't need it, but he was grateful that she lit his path as the night was deep and dark.

It didn't take them long to get back to his car. He hadn't wanted the night to end. The more time he spent around her, the more intrigued and attracted he was to her.

"Would you like to have breakfast with me at the café in the morning before we start work for the day?" he asked on impulse.

To his surprise and pleasure, she tipped her head upward to look at him and then nodded. "Sure, that would be nice," she replied. "I never get breakfast out."

"Then why don't I pick you up here at around seven thirty in the morning," he said, ridiculously pleased she had agreed.

"Okay, I'll be here," she replied. "'Night, Nathan."

"Good night, Angel. Thanks again for tonight. I really enjoyed your friends."

"I'm glad." She turned and quickly melted into the darkness of the night. He got into his car and wondered what in the hell he was doing. Nothing good could come out of him spending extra time with Angel. In a month he'd be gone from here and back to his life in New Orleans. After breakfast in the morning, it was important he keep things strictly professional between them.

SHE HAD NO idea why she had agreed to go to breakfast with him. Angel got home and locked up and then curled up on the sofa to think about the night that had just passed.

She'd been pleasantly surprised by how well Nathan had gotten along with her friends. He'd been friendly and open and she'd thought he'd even won over Louis and Beau by the end of the night, and they were like two tough, overly protective brothers to her.

The next morning, she was at the parking lot early. She loved daybreak when the sun was just rising and painted everything with its gilded glow.

The air smelled fresh and so...green. It was an impossible scent to describe but it fed her very soul. It was definitely the smell of home.

She heard the crunch of his tires before his car came into sight. Her heart did a slight flip in her chest as he parked and stepped out of the car.

"Good morning," he said with a wide smile. "Are you ready for some breakfast?"

"Definitely," she replied.

He quickly walked around to the passenger door and opened it to usher her into his car. She slid in and watched as he walked back around to the driver's side.

The man definitely rocked a pair of jeans. They fit his long legs and firm butt to perfection. The black polo shirt he wore emphasized his broad shoulders and the darkness of his hair.

He got into the car and started the engine, then turned and smiled at her. "You look quite pretty this morning. Pink is definitely a good color on you."

"Thank you," she replied as a rush of warmth filled her. She'd particularly chosen to wear the pink sleeveless blouse this morning because she knew it looked good on her. She'd also put on a bit of mascara, something she rarely did.

"I enjoyed getting to meet your friends last night," he said once they were on their way to the café.

"They all enjoyed meeting you," she replied. "They're a nice bunch, although Beau and Louis have always been a bit overly protective. Jacques is the quieter one of the three."

"Yeah, I noticed."

"I hope you didn't take offense to them and their hundreds of questions."

He shot her a quick smile. "No offense was taken. It's obvious they all care about you very much."

"And I care about all of them," she replied. "So, have you become familiar with the town yet?"

"I know where the hamburger drive-through is located, and the little donut shop. And of course I know where the café is," he replied.

"Ah, I'm sensing a theme here," she said teasingly.

He laughed, the deep rumble resounding in the pit of her stomach. He had such a wonderful laugh. "I do love food. What about you? Do you pick like a bird or do you enjoy a nice big meal?"

"I definitely like to eat," she replied.

They entered the city limits of Crystal Cove. It was a charming place with storefronts painted in pink and yellow and turquoise. There was a grocery store, a dress shop and the official city offices.

There was also a thrift shore and various other little shops that kept the town thriving. Even though the place rarely saw tourists, there was a nice six-unit motel where she knew Nathan was staying. She also knew there were several people who lived full-time at the motel.

As they drove, they talked about the hot, humid weather that always ruled this area in July and small-talked about the people he had met the night before.

It didn't take him long to arrive at the café. He found a place in the café's parking lot and then together they got out of the car and headed for the front door.

The café was always busy in the mornings and even though it was Wednesday, it was no different. Silver-ware clattered and people talked and laughed as they visited with neighbors and family.

The scents of frying bacon and fresh coffee filled the air, along with the fragrance of cooking eggs, grilling vegetables and yeasty biscuits and bakery goods.

They managed to find an empty booth toward the back and settled in. Almost immediately Marianne arrived to wait on them. "Fancy seeing you two here this morning," she said with a bright smile.

"We decided to catch some breakfast together before we get to work," Nathan said.

"Well, you've certainly come to the right place," Marianne replied. "What can I get for you two?"

Nathan ordered a number four special with two eggs, bacon, toast and hash browns and she ordered French toast with bacon. They both ordered coffee and orange juice.

"This is really a nice place," Nathan said once Marianne had left their booth. "I've enjoyed eating my dinners here since I got into town."

"It's owned by a woman named Antoinette LeBlanc. She opened it about twenty years ago and she still very much runs the place and is the main cook."

"The decorations are very nice," he said. "I like the homey feel of it."

It was true that Antoinette had decorated it to feel comfortable and without any nods to the swamp or the town. Hanging on the beige walls were antique kitchen instruments. There was also an oversized wooden fork and spoon painted in copper colors that took up most of one wall.

"It's definitely the most popular place in town. The food is excellent and the prices are reasonable," she replied.

"I've learned that in the past couple of nights when I've had dinner here," he said.

At that moment Marianne returned with their coffee and orange juice and then left them once more to check on her other tables and booths.

"So, tell me more about Angel Marchant," he said.

"What do you want to know?" She took a drink of her coffee.

"I don't know…let's start with this. Where do you see yourself in five years?"

She blinked in surprise. She'd expected an easier question from him. "Oh, I don't know. I'd like to be married and have a baby or two by then. What about you?"

"The same," he replied. "I definitely want a family in the next couple of years."

"How many children would you like?" she asked.

"Two…maybe three."

The conversation was interrupted by Marianne bringing their food. "Thanks, Marianne," Angel said.

"Yes, thanks. This all looks delicious," Nathan added.

"Enjoy," Marianne said as she once again moved away.

"I guess we should dive in while it's hot," Nathan said.

"Definitely," Angel agreed. She grabbed the bottle of syrup and liberally doused her French toast with it while he cut into his over-easy eggs.

"Breakfast is my favorite meal of the day," he said. "I hope you don't mind that I'm a dipper." He picked up his toast and dipped it into the runny egg yolk.

She smiled at him. "I don't mind at all. I say go for it."

They ate for a few minutes in silence. Angel was the one who broke the quiet. "So, is there anything in particular you'd like to see today?"

"No, nothing in particular. I need to take more pictures of the plants. That's what's going to be the most time-consuming," he replied. "There are so many wonderful plants and they each serve a function to keep the swamp healthy. I've got everything written up on them. I'm just lacking the photos."

"I heard you tell the gang last night that you expect this all to take about a month," she said.

"Yes, and while I'd like you to guide me for the period of time I'm here, I certainly understand if you have other responsibilities, especially if those responsibilities revolve around taking care of elderly parents."

"Don't pay attention to what Beau said last night. My parents are perfectly capable of taking care of themselves. However, I do things now to try to make their lives a little easier," she replied.

"So, you're close with your parents. That's nice," he replied.

"I'm very close with them. What about you? Are you close with yours?" she asked curiously.

His eyes appeared to darken in hue. "Unfortunately, my father passed away ten years ago from a heart attack and about eight years ago my mother remarried and she and her new husband moved to Kansas City. We try to stay in touch by phone, but it's just not the same."

"I'm sorry about your father and the way things turned out." There was a sadness in his eyes and Angel fought against the unexpected desire to reach across the table and cover his hand with hers.

"Hey, Angel." Mac Singleton appeared at the side of the booth.

"Hi, Mac," she said and introduced Mac to Nathan. "Mac is the guy I sell all my fish to at the grocery store," she explained. Mac was about Angel's age. He had dark blond hair and hazel eyes and was a pleasant-looking man. Angel had felt for some time that he had a bit of a crush on her, but he'd never asked her out.

"And I've missed seeing you for the last couple of days," Mac replied.

"Don't worry, I've got a basketful of fish to bring in to you tomorrow evening," she replied.

"Good, I'm glad you're coming in tomorrow night and not tonight as today is my day off," he replied. "And now I'll just let you two finish up your breakfast. It was nice meeting you, Nathan." He left their booth and returned to his seat across the room.

"He seems nice," Nathan said.

She nodded. "He's a very nice guy."

Their meals were finished and he gestured to Marianne for their check. "Breakfast is on me," he said as he pulled his wallet from his back pocket.

"Oh, no, I like to pay my own way," she replied in protest.

"Please, allow me to get the tab this morning," he insisted.

"Okay, just this once," she relented, deciding not to argue with him.

Together they left the café and headed back to the swamp. The morning passed quickly as they walked through the thicket and he took pictures.

They small-talked as they walked and she learned he had no siblings, loved fried chicken and also loved the outdoors. As he took his pictures, he explained the plants to her that she'd always taken for granted. He also told her their official scientific names, which she found interesting but knew she'd never remember.

However, there was a wild energy between her and Nathan. Whenever his body accidentally came into contact with hers, she felt a flame clear down to her toes. And she had a feeling he felt it, too. There were several times when their gazes had caught and held for a moment too long.

What was it about this man? Was it just a matter of racing hormones? Was it just because she hadn't been around a man she was attracted to in a very long time? Somehow, it felt deeper than that, but since she'd never felt this way about a man before, she didn't know exactly what to call it.

They knocked off at about four o'clock and made plans for her to meet him in the parking lot the next morning at seven thirty.

She watched him drive away and then turned to head back to her shanty. It was early enough that she could get a little evening fishing in. Maybe sitting on the bank with a fishing pole would give her more clarity about the crazy pull she felt toward Nathan.

She frowned as she walked over her bridge. Something was hanging from her doorknob. As she drew closer, her frown deepened. When she reached her door, she stared at the object.

What in the world? It was a voodoo doll with long dark hair, big green eyes and a tiny knife shoved through its heart. She grabbed it from the doorknob, and then looked around her shanty as chills raced up her back.

Seeing nothing and nobody around, she quickly unlocked her door, went inside and then closed and locked the door behind her. She sank down on the sofa and placed the doll before her on the coffee table.

She didn't believe in voodoo curses, but there were some in the swamp who did. She knew Rosemary made the dolls and sold them from her online store as novelties. But Rosemary certainly hadn't left this for her.

So, who had? And why? All she knew for sure was that it couldn't mean anything good.

Chapter Four

Nathan sat in his motel room and went through the latest photos he had taken. He and Angel had spent the last week together and he'd captured many images of the swamp's beauty.

Each day he spent with Angel he got to know her better and he was having emotions about her he'd never felt before. He lusted for her and every day his lust for her grew hotter and more intense.

But his emotions toward her went much deeper than his lust. He wanted to know about her childhood. He would like to know what made her laugh and cry. He wanted to know all her hopes and dreams.

There was no question in his mind he wasn't falling in love with her. He just wanted to know her better as they were work partners and she was such a unique, strong woman.

Hopefully he would learn some of the things he wanted to know about her tonight. She'd surprised him today by calling him and inviting him to dinner at her place. She said it was to pay him back for the breakfast he'd bought her the other day.

He was definitely looking forward to the evening

with her where they wouldn't be focused on anything swamp and could instead focus on each other.

They hadn't worked today. He couldn't expect her to work with him seven days a week, so they'd agreed to take the day off and meet for dinner at six.

He packed his camera away as he realized it was almost time to leave to meet her at her shanty. Tonight he was walking in on his own without her to guide him. Over the last week he'd paid special attention to the trails and now believed he could make it to her place without her bringing him in.

He'd already showered and shaved and dressed for the evening. When five thirty arrived, he got into his car to drive to the parking lot in front of the main trail.

Each time before he knew he was going to see her, a wave of anticipation coupled with a bit of anxiety swept through him. The anticipation was self-explanatory but the anxiety was more complex.

It was the apprehension of a young man going on his first date, of a man who wanted to please the woman he was with. Finally it was Nathan wanting Angel to like him.

There had been moments over the past week that he'd wanted to point his camera at her. When she'd bent down beneath the Spanish moss, he'd wanted to capture her image. With her green eyes and her long dark hair falling around her shoulders, she'd looked primitive and beautifully wild.

She appeared so strong, so unafraid, and he'd love to capture her beauty and spirit on film. But he would not take a photo of her without her permission and so far he hadn't worked up the nerve to ask her for one.

He arrived at the parking lot and left his car. He had his phone and a small flashlight tucked into his back pocket; the flashlight was for when he left her place later. He also carried with him the stun gun he had bought to protect himself after hearing about the Swamp Soul Stealer.

At least it wasn't dark yet and so it was easier for him to keep his bearings. Entering the swamp was like entering the belly of an unknown beast. It wouldn't be long before nighttime creatures awakened and the daytime animals went to sleep.

The gash on his leg had almost healed up, although he was still using antibiotic ointment and bandaging it, making sure it stayed clean. It didn't hurt anymore, which was a good thing.

He tried to walk slowly, not wanting to arrive at her shanty too early. But the sweet anticipation of spending time with her in her home moved his footsteps faster and faster.

He was ridiculously proud of himself for remembering the directions when her shanty came into view. As he crossed the bridge, he heard the sound of her generator running and smelled something delicious wafting outward.

She answered his knock on the door and greeted him with one of her bright smiles. "Come on in, Nathan," she said and opened the door wider to usher him inside.

"Something smells amazing," he said. Not only did something smell amazing, but as usual she looked incredible. She wore black jeans and a red blouse. The outfit showcased her incredible figure and the color of the blouse looked gorgeous with her dark hair and green eyes.

"Fried chicken. Come sit in the kitchen so I can finish it up," she replied.

"You made fried chicken for me?" He followed her into the kitchen area where the table was set for two. He took a seat there while she moved to the counter where an iron skillet sat on one of the two-top electric burners.

"You told me it was your favorite, so I decided to make it for you and see how mine stacks up to others you've eaten. Want a beer?"

"Sure." He was oddly touched that she'd not only remembered him telling her that fried chicken was his favorite, but that she'd actually gone to the trouble of making it for him.

She pulled a beer from the cooler and handed it to him. "How was your day?" she asked.

"Quiet," he replied. "I had a late breakfast at the café and then spent the rest of the day going through the photos I've taken so far."

"Were you happy with what you had?" She flipped over a couple pieces of the frying chicken and then turned to look at him.

"I'm very happy with most of them. There were a few bad ones in the bunch," he replied and then grinned at her. "That just means I'm not perfect all the time."

She laughed. "Who is? So, what other mistakes have you made in your life besides taking the occasional bad photo?"

He was going to make a joke, but he decided to answer the question seriously. "I fell in love with the wrong woman," he replied.

"Tell me more," she said and then turned back around and began to take the chicken out of the skillet and place the pieces on an awaiting plate.

"There isn't a whole lot to tell. I met her in graduate school and we dated for about seven months. I thought she was my person and we'd get married and start our family together. Then one evening she sat me down and told me she cared deeply about me. She loved me, but she wasn't in love with me and that was the end of that."

She placed the chicken on the table and then paused to gaze at him. "Was your heart broken?"

"Yeah, for a while it was," he admitted. She held his gaze for another long moment and then went to the cooler and retrieved a bowl of coleslaw and a tub of butter and added that to the table. She placed several pieces of bread on a saucer and then sat across the table from him. "Help yourself," she said.

"What about you? Any heartbreaks in your past?" he asked as he got a crispy thigh from the plate.

"I fell in love with the wrong man," she replied.

"Tell me more," he said, echoing back to her what she'd said to him.

She grinned. "Quid pro quo, right?" She paused a moment to take a leg and put it on her plate and then looked back at him. "He lives in town and I dated him for about two years. I thought he was my person and I was expecting a proposal, but instead I found out that on the nights he wasn't here with me, he was with another woman. He was basically leading a double life."

Although her tone was fairly light, he saw a flash of hurt deep in her eyes. "I'm so sorry that happened to you. I'm sure that broke your heart," he said.

"Yeah, it did for a while. Now let's eat up before it gets cold," she said.

He added a heaping spoonful of the coleslaw to his plate and then buttered a slice of bread. Finally he bit into the chicken thigh and an explosion of flavor shot off in his mouth.

"Oh, my God, this chicken is beyond delicious," he said.

Her features lit up. "I'm so glad you like it. The coating is my own recipe. I use it for chicken and some fish."

"Well, whatever it is, it's really good," he replied.

As they ate, they chatted about the places they had been in the swamp and where they planned to go next. The talk turned more humorous as he told her some of his most embarrassing moments when he'd entered the dating pool again. He made her laugh over and over again.

There was something quite intimate about laughing together. He felt more drawn to her than ever. In turn, she told him funny stories about her and her friend group growing up in the swamp.

With the stories came a new depth to their relationship, whatever that was at the moment. All he knew was he liked Angel. He liked her a lot and the more he learned about her, the more taken he was with her.

When dinner was over, he insisted he help her with

the cleanup and then they both got fresh beers and went into the living room where she sat next to him on the sofa.

"Thank you so much for the amazing dinner," he said.

"No problem," she replied. "Did you hear that another woman has disappeared from the swamp and it's suspected she was taken by the Soul Stealer?"

"Yeah, I read that in the paper this morning. Did you know her?"

"Yes, although I didn't know her well. She was a bit younger than me and lived at home with her parents. From what I heard today, she had spent an evening with a friend but never made it back home."

"And the police have no clue who this Swamp Soul Stealer is?" he asked.

She shook her head. "None and I heard today in town that the only person who might be able to help identify him has been placed in a medical coma."

"Colette Broussard, right?"

"Right." She looked at him in surprise.

"I've been doing my homework, and having meals at the café is like being at news central."

She laughed. "Keep in mind not everything you hear at the café is always true."

"I take it all in with a grain of salt, but the one thing I do believe is the Swamp Soul Stealer is dangerous and I worry about you going out and about on your own," he replied.

She released a small dry laugh. "I don't worry so much about the Swamp Soul Stealer right now. I'm more concerned about something a little closer to home."

"What's that?" he asked curiously.

She got up from the sofa and went to the bookcase where she grabbed something off the bottom shelf and carried it back with her. "This was left on my door a few days ago."

She handed him a primitive doll, with long dark yarn for hair and big green eyes. A little knife was stabbed through the heart. He looked up at her with shock.

"This is a nasty piece of work. Do you have any idea who left it for you or why?" he asked.

"Not a clue."

He set the doll on the coffee table and then moved closer to her. "It looks like a threat of some kind," he said.

"I know, but at least nothing else has happened since I got that," she replied. "I asked Rosemary if it was one of hers because she sells the dolls on her online store, but she said it definitely wasn't one of hers. In fact, I asked all my friends about it, but they couldn't figure out who might have left it for me."

"You have to tell me if anything else like this happens," he said.

"Why, what are you going to do about it?" she asked.

"I don't know, but I do know that even though I haven't known you for very long, I care about you," he replied.

"It's funny you say that because I feel the same way about you," she replied and a dusting of pink filled her cheeks. "But of course we need to keep things strictly business between us."

"Of course," he replied and held her gaze. "But I have to confess that I really want to kiss you right now."

A flame appeared to kindle in the depths of her eyes and the tip of her tongue dipped out to dampen her lower lip. A hot fire flickered to life inside him as their gazes remained locked.

"Nathan, I... I really want you to kiss me right now," she said half-breathlessly.

He moved closer to her, tucked a strand of her soft silky hair behind her ear and then lightly touched his lips to hers. He intended the kiss to be brief and soft, but his lips didn't get the memo.

He consumed her mouth with his and when she opened up to him, he dove his tongue in to dance with hers. Her arms encircled his shoulders as he leaned into her.

She tasted of warm beer and hot desire and he would have kissed her forever, but as he felt himself getting very aroused, he reluctantly ended the kiss.

She dropped her arms from around him and sat back. "Do all male scientists kiss as well as you do?" she asked.

He laughed. "I don't know. I've never kissed one. Do all the women in the swamp kiss as well as you do?" He was grateful nothing felt awkward between them.

"I don't know. I've never kissed one," she replied. "Okay, we kissed, and now things need to go back to strictly business between us."

"Of course," he agreed. "And I need to get out of

your hair." He stood and picked up his empty beer bottle to carry it to the trash in the kitchen, but she stopped him.

"Leave it, I'll get it," she said as she also stood.

Together they walked to her door. "Thank you so much for the delicious dinner tonight."

"No problem," she replied. "I'm glad you enjoyed it. Do you need me to walk you out to the parking lot?"

"No, I think I've got it. Are we on for tomorrow morning?" he asked.

"Definitely, same time, same place?"

He nodded. For a long moment they remained close, their gazes locked and a tension building once again between them. "Since we've kind of already blurred the line between strictly business and personal tonight, I wouldn't mind if you wanted to kiss me good-night," she said.

"I would love to kiss you good-night," he replied, surprised by her invitation.

He drew her into his arms and stole her lips with his. Her arms went up around his neck as he pulled her closer and closer against him.

Her body fit perfectly against his own. She opened her mouth to him and their tongues met and swirled together in a deep kiss. He was lost in her. Her scent…her warmth and her lips all combined to dizzy his senses.

He was fully aroused with his want of her. But she had only invited a good-night kiss. With that in mind, he reluctantly pulled his mouth back from hers to end the kiss.

"Good night, Angel," he said as he dropped his arms from around her.

She stepped back from him. "Good night, Nathan. And tomorrow, it's back to strictly business."

"Understood," he replied, and with that he stepped out into the darkness of the night and she closed her door.

He clicked on his flashlight and began the trek back to his car. They could pretend that things were going to be strictly business between them, but he had a feeling with tonight's kisses everything had changed and he was excited to see how those changes played out.

SHE HAD NEVER been that forward with a man before. After Nathan left, Angel sank down on her sofa with her lips still feeling the burning imprint of his.

What on earth had possessed her tonight? Why had she asked him for that second kiss at the door? She could pretend to be confused about it, but the bottom line was she'd just wanted another one of his kisses. Being held in his arms for that brief period of time had felt so good. It had been forever since she'd been held in a man's arms.

There was no question she felt something different with Nathan, something exciting and electrifying. It wasn't just a physical pull, but it was an emotional one as well. He was so easy to talk to and he had a great sense of humor. Her feelings toward him scared her more than a little bit because it had heartbreak written all over it.

She got up and took the voodoo doll back to her

bookshelf. As she did, a shiver walked up her back. She wished she knew who had left it for her and why. Even though nothing else had happened, every time she thought about the voodoo doll she felt as if she was holding her breath, just waiting for something else to occur.

She finally went to bed and awakened just before dawn. She took her pirogue out to run her fish lines as she intended to take the fish she'd caught all week to the café and the grocery store that evening.

Once she was finished with that, she ate a quick breakfast and then at a little after seven o'clock she headed toward the parking lot to meet with Nathan.

She hoped things weren't awkward between them this morning. If she was really smart, she'd cut her losses, quit the tour guide job and never see him again. But the idea of doing that made her heart hurt. She was so enjoying her time with him.

Besides, she told herself it was all about the money. With the cash he was paying her and the savings she'd managed to squirrel away, by the end of this she would have enough to build a bigger, better deck around the shanty and that had been a goal of hers for months.

It's all about the money, she reminded herself as she reached the parking lot. Nathan was already parked there and at the sight of her, he got out of his car with his camera and a bright smile.

Damn him for being so handsome…for looking so fine in his jeans and a navy T-shirt. Damn his blue eyes for being so bright and his smile for being so wonderfully inviting and warm.

"Good morning, oh, faithful tour guide," he said to her.

"Good morning to you, biologist photographer," she replied.

"Now that we know who we are, shall we get started?"

"Follow me," she replied. "I'm going to take you on some new trails this morning."

"Sounds good to me," he said. "I've got my camera ready for anything." They walked for a bit in silence. Thankfully it wasn't an uncomfortable one, but rather a companionable one.

"Did you sleep well last night?" he asked, breaking the silence.

"I did, but I pretty much always sleep well," she replied.

"The one night I stayed at your place it was the croak of the frogs and the water lapping against your stilts that made me sleep like a baby."

"For me, that's the rhythmic lullaby sounds of home," she replied.

"I could definitely get used to that."

"Stick around long enough and you'll fall in love with the swamp," she replied.

"I'm already halfway there," he admitted.

She was grateful that their conversations continued to be light and easy with no talk about what they had shared the night before.

They spoke a little more about the latest news of the woman who had disappeared and was a suspected victim of the Swamp Soul Stealer. There was no more news on the case, and she was still missing.

"Isn't it sad that potentially the most dangerous thing in the swamp is a man," he said when they stopped so he could take photos of the duckweed plants floating in a still pond.

"It's tragic," she replied. "I know Etienne, the chief of police, and his officers have combed the swamp looking for the victims and whoever has them, but the swamp is so dense and vast."

"It would be like looking for a needle in a haystack," he replied. He raised his camera and leaned closer to her to capture images of the frond-like plants. His nearness to her evoked a desire inside her.

It was the desire to touch his warm skin and to feel his lips on hers once again. It was the wish to know all the hopes and dreams in his heart and to share hers with him.

She released a deep sigh as he finished taking photos and straightened up. What was wrong with her? She realized she was in trouble. She was on the verge of being absolutely crazy about a man who would probably only be here for another two or three weeks.

It was wild, she'd known him less than two weeks and yet there was a part of her that felt as if she'd known him forever.

She knew she should stop the free fall, but there was another part of her that wanted to embrace all that was Nathan while he was here and deal later with the potential heartache she might have when he was gone.

That day she showed him a group of wild boars, which he explained to her weren't indigenous to the area. Still, he took photos of the animals along with several other smaller animals that scurried about.

There was nutria, large river rats with Cheetos-orange front teeth and plenty of turtles. They also saw a couple of otters and beavers busily building their homes. All in all, the day was a huge success for him as he got plenty of pictures.

It was late afternoon when they decided to head back. "Angel, I've wanted to ask you something for the last couple of days," he said when they were nearly back to the parking lot.

She stopped and turned to look at him, curious. "What's that?" she asked.

"I was wondering if you'd let me take a couple pictures of you."

She gazed at him in surprise. "Why would you want to do that?"

He smiled, that warm gesture that always made her feel special. "Because you're absolutely beautiful and I'd like to have a few photos to remember my time here with you. In fact, I wouldn't mind including a photo in the book of my intrepid swamp tour guide if you'd allow me to do that."

She frowned at him. "I don't know about being in a book, but if you want to take a few photos of me, I guess I wouldn't mind, but only on one condition."

"And what's that?"

"That you allow me to take a couple pictures of you for me to remember your time here," she replied.

"Sure, if that's what you want," he replied easily.

"Then when do you want to do this?" she asked.

"How about right now?" He raised his camera and began to snap pictures while she stood still, feeling awkward about the whole thing.

After he had taken several, he lowered his camera and smiled at her. "Thank you, you make a lovely model."

"Thanks, now it's my turn." She pulled her phone from her back pocket and took several pictures of him.

When she was finished, she returned her phone to her pocket and they continued their trek back to the parking lot. After telling him goodbye and agreeing to meet the next morning, she headed back to her shanty.

As she walked, all kinds of thoughts tumbled around in her head, all of them concerning Nathan. Each and every moment she spent with him only made her like him more. He seemed to be such a kind, good man and that definitely drew her closer to him. Then there was their physical chemistry. It was definitely off the charts.

She nearly stumbled as a new thought crossed her mind. Was it possible that he was only drawn to her because she was a swamp woman? Something unique and different to be studied? Was it possible she was really nothing more to him than a specimen to be analyzed?

As she reached her bridge, her heart sank as she saw a piece of paper taped on her front door. Now what? She reached the door and pulled off the note.

STAY AWAY FROM THE SCIENCE MAN!

The words were written in bold red marker. She looked around as icy chills crept up her spine. Who had left this for her? Had somebody been watching her and Nathan together? Was somebody watching her right now?

She quickly went inside and locked her door behind her. First the voodoo doll and now the note. Who didn't want to see her around Nathan? And what would happen if she didn't stop seeing him?

Chapter Five

For the first time in a long time, Angel hadn't slept well. The note had unsettled her more than she wanted to admit. Was it merely somebody trying to look out for her or was it a threat of some kind? Coupled with the voodoo doll, it definitely felt more like a threat, but from whom?

She hadn't told Nathan about the note when she'd met him that morning. She knew instinctively that if she did, he would make the decision to stop seeing her for her own safety. And she was the only one who got to make that decision for herself.

It was now almost six in the evening and her lack of sleep weighed heavy on her, but she still intended to make a trip into town to sell the fish she'd caught over the last week. Hopefully that wouldn't take too long so she could catch up on her sleep tonight.

"Angel, you home?" The deep voice came across Angel's bridge and she opened her door to see Jacques, Beau and Louis approaching.

"I'm here," she replied and opened her door wider to allow the men inside.

It wasn't unusual for the three to show up unexpectedly for a visit. "What's happening?" Louis asked as he sank down on the sofa.

"Nothing much," she said. "I was just starting to get things together for a trip into town."

"You taking a haul in tonight?" Jacques asked.

"I am. What are you three doing, besides looking for trouble?" she asked teasingly.

"We just thought we'd check in on you. Have you heard that another woman is missing?" Beau asked.

"I have." Angel sank down in the chair facing the men on the sofa. "And you know that it isn't just women at risk, right? Two men have also disappeared. We're all at risk whenever we go out alone."

"We're big and strong enough to take care of our-selves," Louis said.

"Luka was big and strong, too," she reminded them, referring to their friend who had disappeared. "And he disappeared."

"Yeah, but we worry about you more because you aren't exactly a physical threat to anyone," Beau said.

"I appreciate all the concern, but I can take care of myself," she retorted firmly. "Besides, I'm not spend-ing all that much time alone in the swamp right now."

"What's that photographer guy going to do to pro-tect you? Take a picture of the Swamp Soul Stealer?" Jacques asked, making the other two men snicker.

"He has a name and he's making somebody ner-vous," she replied. She got up from her chair and went to the bookcase where she had placed the note next to the voodoo doll. She picked it up and showed it to her friends.

"Do any of you know anything about this?" she asked.

They all shook their heads. "I don't like this," Beau said. "You don't have any idea who left that?"

"None," she replied.

"What about Remy Theriot?" Louis asked. "We all know he's had a crush on you forever."

Remy lived deeper in the swamp. He was an odd young man who Angel had befriended several years ago. "I haven't seen Remy for months. I doubt very seriously if he's somewhere out there spying on my social life and that he left that note for me."

"Maybe you should take the note's advice," Louis suggested.

She looked at the big handsome man. "Louis Mignot, when has anyone been able to tell me what to do? I'm enjoying my time with Nathan and I'm making good money. I'm not about to do what some damned anonymous person wants me to do."

"Whoa." Louis held his hands up in a gesture of surrender. "It was just a thought."

"Well, think again." She returned the note to the bookcase and then looked at the men. "Now, I'd love to sit and visit with you all, but I need to get my fish ready to take into town."

"We'll help you with that," Jacques replied.

It took a half hour to get the fish on stringers off her back deck and carry them to her pickup truck. In the back of the truck was a very large cooler that she'd already put water in so the fish would stay fresh to go to market.

Normally it would take her much longer to do everything, but tonight with the men's help, it went much smoother and was done all in one trip.

"Thanks, guys," she said when she was ready to get into the truck and take off.

"Hey, I'm sorry if I made you mad earlier," Louis said.

She smiled. "Don't worry, I forgive you."

"He just said out loud what we were all thinking," Beau added. "None of us like the idea of somebody warning or threatening you in any way."

"I appreciate all of you and now I need to get going so I can get back home." She got into the truck, waved a quick goodbye and then took off.

As she drove, she thought of the three men she had just left. She adored them all and would trust any one of them with her life. It was funny, they were all nice-looking but she'd never felt a single romantic spark with any of them.

Despite the note's advice, she had spent much of the day in the swamp with Nathan. He took more photographs as they talked about anything and everything that came to mind. As usual she had completely enjoyed her time with him and the last thing she wanted to mention to him was the note.

There had been several times when the tension between them had been palpable, when their gazes had locked and she had a feeling he was remembering the very hot kisses they had shared. Still, the note bothered her more than she wanted to admit.

She shoved away thoughts of him and the note and

within minutes she was at the grocery store. She parked by the loading dock at the back of the building and then went into the door that led her right next to the butcher's glass enclosure.

Not seeing anyone, she rang the bell that would summon somebody from the back room. Mac Singleton appeared behind the glass and immediately stepped out of the enclosure to greet her.

"You just caught me," he said. "I get off work in a half hour."

"Then I'm glad I came when I did," she replied. "Are you ready to go see some fish?"

"Definitely. My fish supply has gotten low. Let me go find Joey and get my cooler and I'll meet you out by your truck," he said. Joey was a young kid who also worked in the meat and seafood department.

Angel went back outside where the shadows of night were quickly encroaching. She lowered the tailgate of her truck and sat on it to await the men.

It was a beautiful night with a near-full moon rising. The temperature had cooled off enough to be almost pleasant. As she waited, her thoughts once again turned to Nathan.

She still didn't know how she'd come to be so close and to have such feelings for a man in so little time. But something about him had crawled deep into her heart. How was it that when she wasn't with him, she missed him? She'd never felt that about a man before, not even her ex-boyfriend.

She was pulled from her thoughts as Mac and Joey

came outside carrying a large cooler. She opened up hers so Mac could see the fish inside.

"Ah, I see you brought me some beauties," he said as he began transferring the fish from her cooler to his.

"Only the best for you, Mac," she replied teasingly.

"Ha, I know you probably have the best of the bunch stashed away to sell to Antoinette at the café," he said with a laugh. "So, how is life treating you these days? I hear through the grapevine that you're spending a lot of time with that Nathan guy." He talked while he worked, picking out fish and handing them to Joey, who put them in the store cooler.

"I have been spending quite a bit of time with him," she replied as she mentally kept track of the fish he was taking.

"I heard you were working with him. Is it strictly a business relationship?"

"Business and a little more," she confessed.

He straightened up and looked at her intently. "Do you really think it's wise to get into any kind of relationship with him? From what I hear, he isn't going to be in town for long."

She gazed at him in surprise. Mac had never gotten so personal with her before. "No, it's probably not wise," she replied honestly.

"I would just hate to see you get hurt by him."

"That's not going to happen." It was a little white lie. She already knew she was going to be hurt when her time with Nathan was over. Not that she was in love with him or anything that deep, but she would certainly miss their time together.

By that time, Mac had the fish he needed and they negotiated a price. Minutes later she was on her way to the café with plenty of fish left to sell to Antoinette, who was always the bigger buyer.

She'd been surprised by Mac's not-so-subtle probing of her relationship with Nathan. Was it possible she and Nathan were gossip fodder at the café? She supposed it was possible. During the past week she and Nathan had shared another breakfast together at the café before heading into the swamp for work.

She pulled into the alley behind the café where a door was open and a young man, who was obviously on a break, stood smoking. "Will you let Antoinette know that Angel is here?" she asked him.

"Sure." He dropped the last of his cigarette and stepped on it to grind it out. He then disappeared back into the café's kitchen.

A few moments later Antoinette stepped outside. She was a short, squat woman with silver hair pulled into a large bun at the nape of her neck. She was reputed to run a tight ship while being a fair, good employer. She was followed out the door by a tall buff man carrying a large cooler.

"What have you brought for me tonight?" she asked Angel. Despite her age and physical condition, she showed her spryness by jumping up into the bed of the truck.

"You can see for yourself there's a nice variety in there," Angel replied.

"Sam, bring that cooler up here," she said. The big man got into the truck and Antoinette began to pick her fish. When she finished, the two dickered with each other about price. Antoinette was a tough cookie, but Angel was certainly no pushover. They finally came to an agreement. Angel got paid and both parties were satisfied.

Darkness had fallen and Angel was now eager to get home. She hadn't eaten any dinner before she'd left, so she was hungry and tired. Her cooler was now empty and her business was done for the day.

She finally reached home and once she was locked inside, she made herself some fried fish and ate it with a piece of bread and butter.

As she ate, she thought about the day and then the note that had been left for her. Was it possible Mac had left it for her? He'd certainly seemed very concerned about her relationship with Nathan.

Or was it possible one of her friends had left it on her door? Did one of those three men have a secret thing for her? A thing that had become oppressive and controlling?

When she crawled into bed that night, she felt very alone. As the frogs began to croak and the sound of the water lapped outside, she realized she didn't know whom to trust...and that scared her.

NATHAN SAT IN the café and waited for his order to be delivered. He hated eating alone. He hated feeling so lonely. He hated to admit it but he was lonely whenever he wasn't with Angel.

It was more than just being in a town where he didn't really know anyone. It was about his growing feelings for the woman who had helped him when he'd been hurt, for the woman who brightened his days and stirred an intense flame inside him he'd never felt before.

With each day that passed, with each click of his camera, he was getting closer and closer to the end of his time here. There was a touch of sadness growing in him whenever he thought of packing up and leaving Crystal Cove, the swamp and Angel behind.

"Here you go, handsome." Dana Albright was an older woman who almost always waited on him at dinnertime. She set his platter of fried shrimp and mac and cheese before him.

"Thanks, Dana," he replied with a smile. Most evenings he just ordered a burger and fries, but tonight he'd opted for something different.

"Can I top off your iced tea for you?"

"No, I'm good right now."

"Just holler for me if you need anything," she replied and then she left his table.

He was about halfway through his meal when a familiar face greeted him. "Hey, Nathan…mind if I sit with you for a few minutes?" Beau Gustave asked.

"No, I don't mind a bit," Nathan replied.

"So, how are you doing with all your picture-taking?" Beau asked. The man was clad in a dark pair of jeans and a black T-shirt. His dark hair was brushed back from his face, exposing his bold strong features.

"It's all going really well," Nathan replied. At that moment Dana returned to the table.

"Can I get you anything, Beau?" she asked.

"I wouldn't mind a cup of coffee," he replied and

then looked back at Nathan. "As long as you don't mind me hanging out here for a few minutes."

"No, in fact I welcome the company," Nathan replied with friendliness.

"Got it, be right back," Dana said.

"Anyway, I've been getting tons of good photos to use in the book," Nathan said, picking back up the conversation. His mind immediately went to the four photos he'd managed to get of Angel. He'd been grateful that they had come out beautifully.

"That's good," Beau replied.

"Angel has been a very good guide for me. I've been grateful for her help."

"How much more time you think you have here?" Beau asked.

"Maybe a couple more weeks."

Once again, the conversation was interrupted as Dana returned with Beau's coffee. "There you go, honey," she said as she set the cup of dark brew down.

"Thanks, Dana."

"So, then things are going well with our girl, Angel?" Beau asked.

"Things are going great. At this point, I don't know what I'd do without her."

Beau took a drink of his coffee and eyed Nathan over the top of his cup. He lowered his cup slowly but his gaze still held Nathan's intently. "Don't hurt her."

Nathan sat back in his seat, surprised by what sounded like a veiled threat. "Trust me, that's the last thing I'd ever want to do," he replied.

"She's a very special woman and we all love her," Beau said.

"I could see that the night we were all together. Look, Angel has been a godsend to me as far as guiding me around in the swamp, but we both know I'll be leaving here in a couple of weeks."

Beau took another sip of his coffee and then smiled. "As long as you don't intend to take advantage of her in any way, then we're good."

Nathan nodded and held the man's gaze. "We're good."

"Then I'll just let you get back to your meal," Beau said. He stood and without saying another word, he headed for the café's exit.

Nathan watched him go and then picked up his spoon to finish his mac and cheese. As he continued with his meal, he thought about the conversation that had just occurred.

There was no question in his mind now that Beau might have feelings for Angel and he saw Nathan as a threat. But Nathan couldn't be a threat because his time here was limited.

Nathan knew he was more than a little charmed with Angel, but he wasn't sure what she felt about him. Oh, there was no question there was an intense physical attraction between them. He knew she liked him, but it likely was nothing deeper than that.

He'd told Beau the truth; the last thing he wanted was to hurt Angel. But, just like Nathan wasn't in charge of Angel's feelings, neither was Beau. She was a grown woman and surely if she felt uncomfortable with Nathan and the time they were spending together, she would stop seeing him.

It didn't take him long to finish his meal. He told the waitress to add Beau's coffee on his tab. Once he'd paid, he headed back to the motel room. At seven thirty the next morning he was in the parking lot to meet Angel.

He couldn't help the burst of warmth that swept through him at the sight of her. Today she was clad in a pair of jeans and a bright yellow tank top that looked gorgeous against her tanned skin and dark hair. She looked like a beautiful ray of sunshine.

"Good morning," he said.

"Back at you," she replied.

"Are you ready for more exploring today?" he asked as he grabbed his camera and then joined her at the edge of the swampland.

"Always ready," she assured him with one of her bright smiles.

Together they took off, making small talk about the weather, the food in the café and her fish run into town the night before.

As they talked and walked, he snapped pictures along the way. He didn't mention his dinner companion from the night before. He hadn't yet decided if he'd tell her about the conversation with Beau or not.

"How about I take you to my special fishing place and we sit and rest for a few minutes," she said when it was around noon.

"That sounds like a great plan," he agreed. They had been moving pretty much nonstop through the morning and he was ready for a break. "Besides, I'd like to see your special fishing place."

He followed her up another trail and then another and then they broke into a clearing where the bank was a bit high and dry over a quiet small cove of water.

Knobby cypress and tupelo trees rose up all around the shore, dripping with lacy Spanish moss. Insects and fish kissed the surface of the water and birds sang like a melodious choir from the tops of the trees. It was a tranquil place of enormous beauty.

She sank down on the ground and he did the same, sitting close enough that he could smell the wonderful, slightly spicy and mysterious scent of her. "It's really nice here," he said.

"This isn't only my fishing place. Sometimes I come here to sit and think or just to relax."

"It definitely feels like a nice, relaxing place," he replied.

She looked at him curiously. "Do you have a place in New Orleans where you go to just sit and think or relax?"

"Not anywhere as splendid as this. I sometimes go to a little ice-cream shop not far from my place."

"You're an ice-cream man?"

He grinned at her. "Oh, definitely."

"What flavor?"

"Anything caramel. What about you?"

"Chocolate."

"Now you've made me hungry for it. Why don't we go to the ice-cream place in town this evening? We could go to the café for dinner and then have ice cream for dessert."

"That sounds like fun," she agreed, her eyes shining brightly.

"Then I'll pick you up for dinner around six. Will that work?" he asked.

"That will work," she replied with a smile.

"Do you know that your friend Beau is possibly in love with you?" The words blurted out of him before he realized he was going to say them.

"Talk about an abrupt change of subject," she said with a small laugh. "And I don't know where you get your information from, but Beau and I are just good friends. I don't have any kind of romantic feelings toward him."

"I believe he definitely has romantic feelings for you." He went on to tell her about the conversation he'd had with the man the night before in the café. He recognized that he should tell her about the encounter in case she heard something about it from Beau. "In fact, if I was to guess, all three of those men are more than half in love with you."

She laughed again. "And I think you are more than half crazy. Those men love me as friends, but they aren't in love with me."

"Then we'll agree to disagree on that point," he replied easily. Why wouldn't any of those men be half in love with her? Nathan had only known her for less than two weeks and he had feelings for her that he was finding confusing.

The realization of the depths of his feeling for Angel

surprised him. He'd known he was growing closer to her with each day that passed, but it had nothing to do with love. He couldn't fall in love with her because it wouldn't go anywhere. If he loved her, then he was only setting himself up for heartache.

No, he wasn't anywhere near in love with her, he just liked her a lot and wouldn't mind having her in his bed. Friends with benefits; he definitely wouldn't mind that with her.

If he was smart, he'd tell her he didn't need her anymore and he'd stop seeing her. But he wasn't willing to deprive himself of her company and she was a terrific guide through the many trails in the swamp. Apparently on this subject he wasn't a very smart man.

"Shall we get going?" she said after they had been sitting for several minutes in silence.

"Ready." He got to his feet and then held out a hand to her. She took his hand and he pulled her up to her feet. Close...so close, they stood together.

He fought against the wild desire to pull her into his arms and kiss her until the sun set in the sky. Instead, he quickly took a step back from her. "Thanks for sharing your special fishing, thinking and relaxing spot with me," he said in an effort to break the tension that had risen up with their nearness to one another.

"No problem," she replied and then turned and led him back into the tangled trail where he began to once again take photos.

They worked until three and then called it a day. She walked with him to the parking lot where he tossed his camera on the seat and then turned to look at her. He pulled his wallet out and paid her for the day. It was still business when it came to paying her for her services. She quickly tucked the bills into her back pocket.

"I'll meet you back here at six," he said. "And I'm really looking forward to it," he couldn't help adding.

"I'll be here, and I'm really looking forward to it, too," she replied and then as always she turned and quickly disappeared into the swamp.

Chapter Six

Angel returned home and sank down on her sofa, her head filled with a million thoughts. Was it possible Beau really had feelings for her? The whole idea seemed crazy to her. They had been friends forever and he had never made any indication that he wanted anything more from her than her friendship.

Was he overly protective of her? Definitely, as were Louis and Jacques. Ever since she'd moved out on her own, the men had become fierce warriors who watched out for her and her safety.

Surely Nathan had been wrong about Beau. He'd mistaken Beau's overprotectiveness as love. What was more confusing was her feelings toward Nathan.

She didn't want to fall in love with Nathan, but there was no question her feelings for him deepened each and every time they were together. Their conversations were so easy and she loved their shared laughter.

She felt giddy when she was with him, much like she had once felt with her ex. Nothing good had come out of that and nothing good would come out of her falling in love with Nathan.

Still, that didn't stop her from wanting to continue

to see him. She wanted to spend as much time as she could with him. At least she would have wonderful memories of him when he was gone from here.

At five forty, she checked her appearance in her mirror. She wore jeans that she knew fit her like a glove and a coral-colored sleeveless button-up blouse that tied at the waist.

She'd pulled her long hair into a high pony and small gold hoop earrings danced on her ears. Her makeup was minimal, just a little blush and some mascara.

She knew she looked good as she left to go meet Nathan. As she was walking there, she couldn't help but think about the note and the voodoo doll.

STAY AWAY FROM THE SCIENCE MAN!

Who had written it? She certainly wasn't taking the advice and didn't intend to. Still, she felt as if she was holding her breath, waiting for something else to happen. And she had no idea what or where it would come from.

But she lived her own life and made her own decisions and nothing and nobody was going to stop her from what she wanted to do. Life in the swamp could be hard enough without this kind of drama.

When she reached the parking lot, Nathan was waiting for her. He got out of the car with a wide smile. He looked wonderfully handsome in a pair of jeans and a light blue button-up short-sleeved shirt that did amazing things to his eyes and showcased his strong biceps.

"Hi," he said. "You look absolutely gorgeous."

"Thanks, you clean up nicely yourself."

He walked around to the passenger side and opened the door. "Your chariot awaits," he said.

She slid into the seat and then watched as he walked around to get behind the wheel. Part of Nathan's charm was she didn't think he realized just how hot he was. He seemed totally oblivious to the fact.

"Are you hungry?" he asked when he got in the car.

"Always," she said with a laugh.

"I like that about you," he replied. "My ex was one of those women who only picked at her food and made me feel guilty for what I was eating."

"You'll never have that problem with me. As you know, I love food and I encourage you to eat however much of whatever you want," she replied.

"Like I said, I definitely like that about you." He shot her a quick smile. "So, anything new since last time I saw you?"

"I can report that nothing new happened in the last two hours. I sat on the sofa for a while and then started to get ready to go out," she replied. "What about you?"

"Also nothing new to report. I watched television for about an hour and then I started getting ready to pick you up."

"Are we getting boring?" she asked teasingly.

"That's us…just a boring old couple going to dinner together."

"Actually, in all the time I've spent with you, I've never found you boring," she admitted.

"I can say the same. I find everything about you and your lifestyle here in the swamp interesting."

Once again she wondered if she was just another swamp specimen to be studied by him. Did he really see her for the woman she was or as a foreign species to be analyzed? She hoped it wasn't that, but she couldn't know for sure what went on in his head.

She shoved the troubling thought aside, intent on just enjoying the evening with him. It didn't take them long to get to the café and be seated at a booth toward the back.

As usual the place buzzed with conversations and people laughing and eating. It smelled like a cornucopia of different mouthwatering flavors.

"I've eaten here most every night and have yet to get a bad meal," he said as he offered her a menu and then took one for himself.

"I haven't eaten here very often but everyone always raves about the food."

"Most nights I just get a burger and fries, although I do like the fried shrimp, too. But I'm thinking of something different tonight," he said.

For a moment they both studied the menus in silence and then he closed his. She looked at hers for a moment longer and then also closed hers.

At that moment a pleasant older woman Angel didn't know came up to the side of the table. "Evening, Nathan," she said in greeting and offered Angel a friendly smile.

"Evening, Dana," he replied and then looked at Angel. "Angel, this is Dana Albright, waitress extraordinaire. And Dana, this is Angel Marchant."

"Nice to meet you, Angel," she replied. "Now, what can I get for you two this evening?"

"I'd like the fish platter," Angel said.

"And I'll take the chicken fried steak," Nathan added. They both ordered iced tea and then Dana left their booth.

"Even with all the options on the menu, you still choose to have fish," he said.

She smiled. "What can I say? I love fish."

"So, you can take the fisherwoman out of the swamp, but you can't take the fish out of her mouth."

She laughed. "I think you just butchered that saying."

He grinned, that special grin of his that always made her heart beat just a little bit faster. "I think you're right."

Dinner was very pleasant. They talked about the things they'd seen in the swamp that day and about some of the charming stores in town.

"How does Rosemary manage to work an online shop from the swamp?" he asked, curious. "Does she have a generator big enough to run a computer?"

"No, there's a little shop off Main Street that offers internet services for a small daily fee. There are several people from the swamp who work from there," she explained.

"Interesting."

As dinner continued, he made her laugh with more stories of his time as a young teacher and biologist, and she returned with more funny stories about growing up in the swamp with her friends.

The food was delicious and all too quickly the meal

was done. "I hope you saved plenty of room for ice cream," he said as he motioned to Dana for their check.

"Definitely," she replied as she opened her purse.

"I don't know what you think you're doing, but stop it right now," he said with mock sternness.

"I've told you before that I like to pay my own way," she protested.

"Angel, I invited you to dinner and for ice cream tonight, so I pay. If you want to repay me, then cook me another meal."

She closed her purse. "Okay, you got it. Tomorrow night plan on dinner at my place."

"Sounds perfect," he replied with one of the smiles that warmed her down to her very toes.

Minutes later they walked out of the café. Although warm and humid as usual, it was a nice clear night. The sinking sun left behind a faint hue of pink and orange that added to the beauty of the skies.

"You want to drive to the ice-cream shop or should we walk?" he asked.

"We can just walk. It's only a block away. That is if you can walk after that huge meal you just scarfed down," she said teasingly.

"Ha, I noticed you cleaned your plate, too."

Together they began to leisurely walk side by side. They had only taken a couple of steps when he reached out and took her hand in his. "Do you mind?"

She smiled at him. "I don't mind at all." His hand was big and strong around hers and it just felt right.

They walked at a leisurely pace, noting the businesses they passed along the way. "I spent way too much money in that place," he said as they walked by a clothing store. "They had some really nice shirts and slacks that I decided I couldn't live without."

He looked at her. "You don't strike me as a woman who cares much about always buying new clothes, although the blouse you're wearing tonight looks beautiful on you."

She felt her cheeks warm. It had been a very long time since a man had complimented her and it felt wonderful. "Thanks, and no, I don't care too much about buying new clothes. I have some nice things in my closet if I need them, but there aren't too many places to go in the swamp where you need to be dressed up."

"You look great in just your jeans and a tank top," he said.

"My, my, Mr. Merrick, careful or you're going to swell my head with all your compliments," she said with a small laugh.

By that time they had reached Bella's Ice Cream Parlor. It was a small shop with a long counter, behind which there were round cartons of all flavors of ice cream. There were four small high-top round tables and also a small counter against one wall for customers to sit. The only customers inside at the moment were a teenage boy and girl seated at one of the tables.

"Hi, welcome to Bella's," a petite blonde greeted them from behind the counter with a cheerful smile. "What can I get for you folks this evening?"

"I'd like chocolate ice cream in a waffle cone," Angel said.

"And I'd like the caramel drizzle in a cup with caramel sauce on top," Nathan said.

It didn't take them long to get their treats and settle in at one of the tables. "Now this is a way to finish up an evening," she said.

"I totally agree," he replied as he dug his spoon into his cup. "Do you treat yourself to ice cream often?"

"Almost never," she replied. "I'll occasionally buy one of those little cups at the grocery store, but it's too hard to keep in the ice cooler for long."

"And I imagine it would be far too expensive to run a generator and a refrigerator full-time."

"Yes. Unfortunately that's one drawback of living in the swamp, but I get by fine with my cooler."

His gaze held hers for a long moment. "And you would never consider moving out of the swamp?"

"Never. The swamp is in my blood, in my very soul. I'm where I belong and where I'll always be," she replied firmly, wondering why he'd even asked the question.

They finished their ice cream and then headed back to his car. The darkness of night had fallen and stars twinkled in the skies.

Once again, he took her hand in his as they walked back. It didn't feel like business with him, rather it felt as if they were a couple exploring a more personal relationship. And she didn't want it to stop.

She was almost disappointed when they reached his car and she knew their night together was coming to an end. "Is there anything in particular you'd like on the menu for tomorrow night?" she asked when they were almost back to the parking lot.

"Whatever you want to make. I'm sure whatever it is, it will be delicious."

"Keep those high hopes, young man," she replied, making him laugh. Oh, she loved the sound of his deep laughter. She'd like to have her ear on his bare chest when he laughed. She could only imagine the deliciously deep and rumbling noise it would make.

Within minutes they were back at the parking lot. They both got out of the car and he walked with her to the beginning of the trail into the swamp.

"I really enjoyed this evening," he said as he stepped closer to her.

"I really enjoyed it, too. Does six o'clock sound good for tomorrow night?" She felt a little breathless by his nearness and the glowing shine in his eyes that was visible in the moonlight.

"That sounds perfect," he replied. "Angel, can I kiss you good-night?"

"I'd like that." Her entire body tingled as he took her into his arms. His lips captured hers and she immediately opened her mouth to invite him to deepen the kiss.

When he did, chills of delight danced through her. Kissing and being kissed by Nathan was a special kind of magic. A hot, sweet desire rose up inside her. It was the desire for him to touch her bare skin, for her to touch his.

At that moment he broke the kiss and dropped his arms from around her. "Since you're cooking for me tomorrow night, maybe you'd like to take tomorrow off."

"Are you sure that's okay with you?"

"It's more than fine with me. I can take the time to go through the photos I've taken in the last week or so. I'll just see you tomorrow night," he replied. "Good night, Angel."

"'Night, Nathan," she replied as she tamped down the desire that had risen up so quickly inside her with the kiss. She turned and headed up the trail that would eventually take her home. She heard the sound of Nathan's car driving off and thought about the desire that had kicked up so high in her at his kiss.

Did she want to make love with him? Absolutely. Was it a good idea for her to make love with Nathan? Absolutely not. She had a feeling all she'd have to do was give him a little more encouragement and he'd be in her bed. She'd tasted his desire for her in the kisses they had shared.

She stopped in her tracks as she heard a loud crashing coming from someplace behind her. She turned in her tracks and gazed behind her. In a shaft of moonlight casting down amid the leaves overhead, she saw a man clad all in black and wearing a ski mask and rushing toward her.

Wha...what the hell? Acting purely on survival instinct, she turned and ran, at the same time fumbling at her waist for her little sister. A loud roar of what sounded like pure rage bellowed from the man. Animals scurried away from the trails as sheer terror gripped Angel.

With her knife gripped tightly in her hand, she ran blindly through the trails. The back of her throat threatened to close up and deep gasps escaped her as she raced for her very life.

Tree limbs tried to grab at her and the Spanish moss half blinded her as she sped ahead. None of that mattered as the crashing noise continued to follow her.

Who was it? Who was chasing her and why? Questions flew frantically through her brain. Oh, God, was it the Swamp Soul Stealer trying to make her his next victim? Would Nathan show up in the morning only to realize she had disappeared...vanished without a trace?

It didn't really matter who it was; the fact that he wore a ski mask meant he intended harm. The last thing she wanted was to lead the person to her shanty and so she raced in the opposite direction.

Her breaths became deep pants and she struggled to keep the screams that wanted to be released inside her. She could feel him getting closer and closer. She imagined she could feel his hot breath whispering on the back of her neck.

She was afraid she couldn't run fast enough to stay in front of him and instead she began to frantically look around for a place to hide. If she could just lose him for a minute...just long enough so she could dive into a thicket and pray he wouldn't find her there.

The deeper she ran into the swamp the less moonlight was able to pierce through the thick foliage overhead. At the moment the darkness was her friend and when she got the opportunity where she didn't believe he could see her, she dove into a thick tangle of woods and vines. She pulled herself into the smallest ball she could make and sat perfectly still.

Desperately she tried not to move, to not even breathe. Her hand gripped her little sister tightly. She didn't want to have to use it. The last thing she wanted was a personal confrontation with whoever was after her. Why? Why was this happening? Who could it be?

Her muscles remained tense, ready to spring into action in a second if necessary. There was a sudden stillness. Although she couldn't see him, she heard him. His deep ragged breathing filled the air, letting her know he was very close to where she hid.

Her body wanted to shiver in sheer terror, but she squeezed her eyes closed and suppressed it, knowing that any kind of involuntary movement or sound meant he would find her. And then what? Oh, God, what did he want? What did he intend to do to her if he did find her?

Move away! she screamed inside her head. *Please, move away!* He was so close to her. He was just standing on the trail as if waiting for her to do something to show herself.

After several agonizing minutes, he continued to crash through the trail away from her. He roared once again, the animalistic sound raising the hairs on the nape of her neck and along her arms.

As he continued to move away from her, she rose from her position and ran toward her shanty. Even though she tried to run as quietly as possible, deep sobs began to escape her. She stuffed the back of her hand into her mouth in an effort to staunch them.

Still, the sobs continued as she finally reached the bridge that carried her to her front porch. She unlocked the front door with trembling fingers and then flew inside, quickly locking the door after her.

She still gripped her knife tightly in her hand as she went to her front window and gazed out into the night. Would he find her here? Did he know where she lived? Sobs continued to escape her, along with deep pants for air.

She had no idea how long she remained at her window with sheer terror a living, breathing thing inside her. Finally, as the minutes ticked by and her breathing started to return to normal, the horror began to ebb somewhat. But it certainly didn't go away.

Had it been the Swamp Soul Stealer after her tonight? Or did this have something to do with the voodoo doll and the note?

At this point it didn't matter. All she knew was she'd never been so afraid in her life. It felt as if a rageful animal had been unleashed in the swamp and she'd been the target. Why? And who had it been?

She remained awake for a very long time and then finally fell into a troubled sleep on her sofa with her little sister still gripped in her hand.

HE RAN THROUGH the swamp toward his home, his rage an animal bursting from his veins, from the very heart of him. The bitch. He'd watched her and the intruder kiss. He'd seen the way she'd leaned into him and he'd pulled her intimately close to him. The traitorous bitch.

The minute he'd seen them, a sharp, wild anger had risen up inside him. He'd already warned her. He'd left her the voodoo doll and the note to warn her away from the man.

Had she forgotten she was swamp? He loved her. He'd been in love with her for a while and she was supposed to be his. They had always been destined to be together. She had even promised she was his girl forever.

But now his love for her had turned to complete disgust…to absolute hatred. A new rage roared through him as he thought of her and the science man kissing so intimately. She was not worthy of his love.

He wasn't sure what he would have done to her tonight if he'd caught up with her, but it wouldn't have been good. He could have shown up at her shanty and made her pay for her disloyalty, but he'd give her one last chance to change her ways and if she didn't, then she would die in the swamp she professed to love.

Chapter Seven

Angel awakened later than usual the next morning and for the first time in years she'd decided not to do a fish run. She hated to admit it but the fear from the night before still had a firm grip on her.

She went outside to take a shower in the structure she'd built on the back deck. She collected rainwater for the showers she took and the system worked out quite well. At least the back deck couldn't be reached unless somebody came through her shanty or approached by water, so she felt safe there.

After the shower, she pulled on fresh clothes and then placed her knife back in the sheath around her waist. She then made herself breakfast and as she picked at the eggs she had made, her thoughts raced with the horrifying events of the night before.

Who had chased her? Who was the man beneath the ski mask? His deep roars of rage had made the entire swamp shiver in fear. Did the monster come out in the daytime or only at night?

She had a feeling he needed the darkness to completely hide his identity, although if he wanted to kill her or make her disappear, then her knowing his identity wouldn't have mattered.

Too bad Colette Broussard was still in her coma. She was potentially the only person who might be able to identify the Swamp Soul Stealer.

Angel certainly couldn't identify the person who had chased her last night. Between the darkness and the ski mask, it had been completely impossible. She wasn't even sure she could give a good description of his body type. In the terror of the night, he'd seemed huge…bigger than life.

Should she call Etienne and make a report of what had happened? At this point, what could the lawman do about it? She had no real description of the man, and it was over now. She turned it over for several minutes in her mind and in the end she decided not to call the police.

She spent the morning dusting and cleaning up the place. At least Nathan would be here this evening and she always felt safe when she was with him.

Just after noon she was about to head out to go into town when Shelby and Rosemary dropped in. "Hey, girlfriend, it's been a while since we've checked in with each other," Shelby said as she sank down on the sofa.

"Yeah, you've been so busy with your new boyfriend," Rosemary added with a sly grin.

"Nathan's not my boyfriend," Angel protested with a small laugh. She sat in the chair facing her friends. "But I'm really enjoying working with him and I am making him dinner tonight," she confessed.

"Just say it, Angel," Shelby said. "You're crazy about

the man. It's evident every time you even just say his name."

"What difference does it make how I feel about him. He'll be gone in two weeks or so." A wave of depression threatened to sweep through Angel. She didn't even want to think about when it came time to say goodbye to him. He'd filled her days with so much laughter and good conversation.

"That totally stinks," Rosemary said softly.

"It is what it is. I knew the timeline all along," Angel replied.

"So, what's on the menu for tonight?" Shelby asked.

"I don't know yet, I need to make a trip into town and go to the grocery store."

"Those smothered pork chops you make are totally yummy," Shelby said.

"Thanks, maybe I'll make those for him," she replied.

"Angel…what's up with you? You don't have your normal energy level or cheerful smiles today," Rosemary observed.

"I had a rough night," Angel confessed, and then told her friends about being chased through the swamp the night before.

"Oh, my God," Shelby said once Angel was finished. "You must have been absolutely terrified.

"I was." Angel fought off a shiver that threatened to creep up her spine at the memory of just how terrified she had been. "I was terrified."

"Do you think it was the Swamp Soul Stealer?" Rosemary asked, her eyes wide.

"Either that or it was the person who left the voodoo doll and the note for me," Angel replied.

"The note? What note," Shelby asked, curious.

Angel got up and grabbed the note from the bookcase and then set it on the coffee table for them both to see.

"When did you get this?" Shelby asked.

"It was left on my door a few nights ago."

"Have you talked to Etienne about all this?" Rosemary asked.

Angel shook her head. "With everything else he has on his plate, I really didn't want to bother him with this. Besides, all I can tell him is I was chased through the darkness by an unknown man. What can he do about that?"

"Then what are you going to do?" Shelby said, her concern rife in her voice.

Angel shrugged her shoulders. "What can I do about it? I'll just have to be careful when I go out and about, especially after dark."

"Why don't you invite one of the men to stay here with you for a while?" Rosemary asked. "You know any one of them would drop everything and do that for you."

"I know that, but I don't want any of them here in my personal space," Angel replied. She didn't want to say that she wasn't sure she trusted them anymore.

"I understand that," Shelby replied. "I love all of them, but I wouldn't want to spend 24/7 with any of them."

"I wouldn't mind spending that kind of time with Beau," Rosemary said with a sigh.

Both Angel and Shelby looked at her in surprise. "You have a thing for Beau?" Shelby asked.

Rosemary nodded. "I've had a thing for him for a long time now."

"Have you let him know how you feel?" Shelby asked.

"No. I'm still trying to get my nerve up," Rosemary replied. "Eventually I'll pick the time and place to let him know."

"You should tell him how you feel about him soon," Angel replied. "Now, what are you two doing out and about today?" Angel asked.

"We're both off work today and so we decided to go into town and have lunch at the café. We stopped by to see if you wanted to go with us, but I guess that's a firm no," Shelby said.

"That's definitely a no," Angel replied. "Next time," she added.

The three continued to talk for about another half hour or so and then they left. Angel walked out with them to head into town.

She breathed a sigh of relief as she reached her pickup. The swamp once again felt friendly this afternoon. She now knew she needed to make sure she got everything done that needed to be done during the daylight hours whenever possible.

When darkness fell, the swamp was not her friend. She wasn't sure what she'd do about taking her fish into town to sell. Both Mac and Antoinette preferred she come later in the evenings to meet with them. But she couldn't think about that right now. In fact she refused to think at all about the night that had just passed.

All she wanted to focus on was the fact that Nathan would be at her place this evening and she wanted to cook him a great meal. Twenty minutes later she pulled up and parked at the grocery store.

She picked up a small bag of potatoes, then added a can of corn to her basket. She then went to the dairy section and grabbed a small bottle of milk. She had decided she'd make the pork chops that Shelby had mentioned, along with mashed potatoes and corn.

Hopefully Nathan liked pork. She knew from some of the conversations they'd shared that he was a man who liked almost everything when it came to food. The only thing she'd heard him say that he didn't like was brussels sprouts, and she was in total agreement with him on that. She didn't like them, either.

The last place she went in the store was to the butcher area. Mac saw her through the glass and stepped out to greet her.

"Aren't you looking pretty this afternoon," he said in greeting.

"Thanks, Mac," she replied with vague surprise. It was the first time he'd ever said something about the way she looked.

"Is there anything in particular you're looking for today?" he asked.

"I need three nice-looking thick pork chops," she replied. She'd decided to buy three in case Nathan could eat more than one.

"Three, huh. That's a big order for you," he observed.

"I'm having a guest tonight for dinner."

"Let me guess, you're having that city, science man

for dinner," Mac said with a faint hint of disgust in his voice.

"That's right," she replied.

Mac held her gaze intently. "Just don't forget where you came from, Angel."

"Don't worry about me, Mac." What she wanted to tell him was to stay in his own lane and mind his own business, but she didn't because she did sell to him and she wanted to maintain that relationship.

"Let me look in the back and see if I can find you three nice pork chops." He disappeared into the butcher area behind the glass.

Angel released a deep sigh. Why did anyone care that she was spending her time with Nathan? They all knew he would only be here for a short amount of time and it wasn't like she was going with him when he left. She was just enjoying his company while he was here and that was her right and her choice.

It hadn't been lost on her that Mac had called Nathan that "science man." Those were the very same words that had been left on the note she received.

Was it possible Mac had left the note for her? Even though Mac had an apartment in town, he had grown up in the swamp and certainly knew his way around there.

How pathetic was it that she would even suspect the butcher she'd done business with for years of putting a warning note on her front door? It proved to her that she really had no idea who to trust. Except Nathan. She completely trusted him.

"Here we go," Mac said as he returned to where she

waited. He handed her a package of three nice thick pork chops.

"Thanks, Mac. These look really great." She placed them in her basket. "I'll see you later."

"Angel, be careful when you're out and about," he said.

"I always try to be," she replied, once again unsettled by him.

She finished up the shopping and the last thing she did was buy a block of ice for her cooler. She loaded everything up and then headed for home.

The inability to know whom to trust was almost as frightening as her race through the swamp last night. Equally as unsettling was the fact that the one man she trusted, the one man she felt safe with would be gone in a very short period of time and she would be all alone.

As USUAL, as Nathan got ready to go to Angel's for the evening, a sweet anticipation rushed through him. If somebody had told him six months ago that he would have such deep feelings for a woman from the swamp, he would have told them they were crazy.

Angel had been such a surprise to him. With the end of his time here quickly approaching, along with the anticipation of seeing her again, there was a growing sadness inside him as well.

He was definitely going to miss her when he left. He would miss her smiles and her laughter. He would miss the conversations they had about anything and nothing. He didn't know how long he would mourn for what might have been if they hadn't been from two such very different worlds. He would definitely mourn for the deep friendship they had built.

He parked in the lot just before five thirty. Knowing he was early, he decided to sit and wait about ten minutes before walking into her shanty.

There was no question he'd grown to love this beautiful yet potentially dangerous place. The beauty of the swamp was apparent no matter where you looked. It was only when you delved deeper beneath the surface that you recognized the dangers.

Along with the gators that hid in dark waters, there were also lots of snakes, some harmless and some poisonous. But he knew how to stay away from both dangers and so for him the beauty far outweighed the dangers.

There was also a real peace inside Angel's shanty, a peace he'd never felt before. It was as if the world outside didn't exist. Time stood still when he was with her in her cozy home. Suddenly he couldn't wait any longer. He grabbed the bouquet of flowers he'd bought for her off the passenger seat and then got out of his car.

He'd been in the grocery store buying a couple of bags of chips for snacks in his motel room when he'd seen the bright, colorful bouquet of daisies. The flowers were dyed a hot pink, bright yellow, turquoise and neon green.

It had been an impulse buy because they had instantly reminded him of Angel. Bright and vivid and fun... He just hoped she liked them and understood it wasn't a romantic gesture from him. He quickened his steps as her shanty came into view.

He headed across her bridge and then knocked on her door. She answered almost immediately and he held out the bouquet. "I saw these today in the floral section of the grocery store and I immediately thought of you."

"Oh, Nathan. Thank you, I absolutely love them." She took the bouquet from him and opened the door wider. Once he was inside, she closed and locked the door behind him. "Let me just get something to put these in."

"Something smells absolutely delicious in here," he said and followed her into the kitchen area.

"That would be your dinner," she replied. She placed the flowers on the table where no plate was set and then looked under the sink. She pulled out a tall clean jelly jar. "I don't have any real vases. Nobody has ever bought me flowers before."

"Really? Now that's a real sin," he replied, genuinely surprised.

"Have a seat," she said and gestured to the table. "Dinner will be ready in about fifteen…twenty minutes." She got a pair of heavy-duty scissors from a drawer and then began to trim down the long-stem flowers and arrange them in the jelly jar.

It took her only minutes and then she added water and set the arrangement in the center of the table. "They look beautiful. Thank you again, Nathan."

"It's my pleasure," he replied.

She threw away the stems she had cut and then moved to her stovetop burner where a covered skillet was on one burner and potatoes were boiling on the other one. As usual, Angel looked beautiful.

She wore jeans and a sleeveless button-up pink-and-white-flowered blouse. Her hair was a rich dark curtain around her shoulders and his fingers itched to lose themselves in it.

However, something seemed a little off with her this evening. The smiles she offered him as they talked moved her lips upward, but didn't quite reach her eyes the way they normally did.

He sensed something was wrong but didn't think it was his place to probe. Hopefully she would tell him if it was something important and she thought he needed to know. In the meantime, all he could do was try to bring out more real smiles from her.

"Genuine mashed potatoes? I'm so impressed," he said as she began to beat the potatoes with butter and milk.

"Is there any other kind?" she asked.

"I usually get the ones in a package that you add to boiled water."

She looked at him and turned up her nose. "Ugh, that sounds positively awful."

He laughed. "Actually, they aren't that bad, but nothing beats the real deal."

She opened a can of corn, poured it into a saucepan and then put it on the burner where the potatoes had been. She then opened the lid to the skillet and stirred whatever was inside.

"So, how has your day been?" he asked.

"Okay. Shelby and Rosemary came by to get me to go to lunch with them at the café, but I declined. I knew I had an important dinner to cook tonight."

"You do realize you could have simply served me buttered bread and I would have enjoyed it as long as we were eating it together."

She smiled and this time the sparkle was back in the depths of her eyes. "I would at least put a piece of bologna on the buttered bread, but tonight smothered pork chops are on the menu."

"How did you know that's a favorite of mine," he replied with a grin.

She laughed. "It's funny how everything I cook for you is your favorite. I hope you're hungry because I made plenty."

"I'm hungry. I skipped lunch today because I knew I'd be eating well tonight."

She grabbed the plates off the table and began putting the food on them. Once they were both ready, she set one plate in front of him and then sat opposite him at the table with a plate before her.

"This looks absolutely delicious," he said.

"I hope it tastes as good as it looks."

"I'm sure it will." It took him only a couple of bites to taste how good it was. The pork chop was tender and flavorful with the gravy that covered it. "You are really a good cook, Angel," he said.

"Thanks. I don't cook much but I owe everything I know about it to my mother, who cooked good meals for my father every evening."

"How are your parents doing?" he asked.

"They're doing okay. I haven't been by to see them lately, but I've spoken to them on the phone a couple of times."

"That's good, and by the way, I didn't tell you how pretty you look tonight."

She smiled at him. As always, the smile warmed his heart. "Nathan, you're very good for a girl's ego."

He returned her smile. "I just call them like I see them."

As they ate, the conversation flowed easily, as it always did when they were together. As the meal continued and they laughed about a variety of things, her smiles were more normal as her eyes sparkled with her amusement.

Whatever was bothering her didn't seem to be bothering her anymore and he was grateful for that. He wound up eating two of the pork chops along with plenty of mashed potatoes and corn.

"I'm absolutely stuffed," he said as he got up from the table to help her with the cleanup. "You might have to roll me out of here when it's time for me to leave tonight."

"Ha, there's nothing round about you," she replied.

They continued to talk as they finished up with the dishes. As he stood next to her and helped her, he wished he could do this every night. Just the simple task done together was a pleasure.

She grabbed them a couple of beers and then they moved into the living room where they sat down on the sofa. Immediately he felt her energy change. The sparkle was once again gone from her eyes and she released a deep sigh.

"What's going on, Angel?" he asked softly.

"Oh, nothing." She took a drink of her beer and averted her gaze from him.

"Angel, don't tell me nothing when there's obviously something bothering you. You should know by now that you can tell me anything." He scooted closer to her. "Talk to me, honey."

She set her beer down on the coffee table and then looked at him, her beautiful green eyes appearing darker than usual. "Last night when I left you, I was chased through the swamp by a man dressed all in black and wearing a ski mask."

He stared at her in growing horror as she continued to tell him about the howls of rage and her frantic run to escape the person.

"I was so scared," she said as her eyes welled up with tears. "Nathan, I… I've never been so terrified in my entire life."

He reached for her and she came willingly into his arms. He held her tight as she began to cry in earnest. He stroked up and down her back while murmuring reassuring words.

"It's okay. You're safe now," he said.

She nodded and clung to him, still weeping against his neck. Meanwhile, as he soothed her, his mind raced. Had it been the Swamp Soul Stealer who had chased her the night before?

Who else could it have been? He couldn't imagine Angel having any enemies in the swamp. It had to have been the monster that everyone feared.

Had she simply been a convenient target walking home in the dark? Or had she been specifically targeted? This thought shot fear for her straight through his heart and soul. Thank God she had gotten away. Thank God she was here and relatively unharmed.

"I… I'm sorry. I'm s-so sorry." She finally pulled away from him and swiped her cheeks in obvious embarrassment.

"Please don't apologize. You obviously needed that cry," he replied gently. He reached out and tucked a strand of her hair behind her ear so he could better see her features.

"I guess I did," she replied with a half laugh.

"Have you told anyone else about this?" he asked. "Did you call the police?"

She shook her head. "No, I know there's really nothing Etienne can do about it now, but I did tell Shelby and Rosemary about it when they stopped by earlier."

"And I'm sure they were very worried about you," he replied.

"They were, but it's over and done with now and as you said, I'm safe and that's all that matters." Her eyes still appeared dark and haunted with residual fear.

"I have a suggestion for you," he began.

"And what's that?" She looked at him curiously.

"You let me move in here with you so you never have to be out in the dark alone again for as long as I'm in town." He held his breath as her eyes widened in stunned surprise.

Chapter Eight

Angel stared at Nathan, shocked not only by his suggestion, but also by the fact that she was actually considering it.

"Think about it, Angel," he continued as he leaned forward. "I can sleep here on the sofa and I'd try to stay out of your way as much as possible. But I'd be here when you have to go out. You said yourself that there was safety in numbers and I don't feel right leaving you here all alone and so vulnerable right now."

He was definitely making a hard sell. What she also thought about was she'd never have to tell him goodbye at the end of the day. She could enjoy his company all the time. Of course, he would sleep on the sofa, but he'd be here with her throughout the darkness of the night.

It would probably make it all the more difficult when he had to leave for good, but she didn't want to think about that right now. With the terror of the night before still deep in the back of her throat, she slowly nodded her head.

"Okay," she said.

"Really? You'll let me be here for you?"

"Nathan, I've never needed anyone in my entire life,"

she said. "But I have to admit having you here will make me feel better…safer. Hopefully my fear will pass soon and I'll be fine on my own once again. Still, I know there will be times I have to be out after dark, mostly on the evenings when I make fish runs."

"From now on I'll be by your side on those nights and on any other nights you have to be out," he replied. His eyes shone with the light that always made her feel special. "Angel, I actually feel honored that you'll allow me to do this for you."

She laughed as an enormous relief rushed through her. "You won't feel so honored when you see me first thing in the morning after I've just rolled out of bed."

His eyes sparked with something dangerous and delicious. "I actually look forward to that." She broke eye contact with him as a wave of heat swept through her. This was about her safety, not about her hormones.

"So, when do you want me to make the move here?" he asked.

She gazed at him once again. "How about sometime tomorrow?"

"Okay, shall we say about noon? It won't take me long to pack my bags and check out of the motel."

"That sounds perfect." Now that she'd agreed to let him be here, she couldn't wait for it to happen as soon as possible.

"Now, I'd better get out of here before you change your mind about me staying here with you." He stood and finished the last of his beer.

She got up as well to walk him to the door. When

they reached it, a sudden fear for him gripped her. "Do you have your stun gun with you?"

He pulled it out of his pocket. "I never travel without it."

"Keep it out until you get back safely to your car."

He leaned closer to her. "Now that my leg is pretty much healed up, I can definitely run like hell. Don't worry about me, Angel. I'll be fine and I'll be here at noon tomorrow. Now, can I kiss you good-night?"

"I'd like that," she replied. She wanted to be held in his arms just one last time before he left for the night.

He gathered her close, but instead of the hot kisses they had shared in the past, his kiss was gentle and infinitely filled with a caring and warmth she hadn't even known she needed.

"I'll see you tomorrow," he said as he released her. "And don't go outside tonight."

"Don't worry. I have no plans to be out tonight," she assured him.

It was only when he was gone that she realized she still hadn't shown him the note she had received. She sank down on her sofa and grabbed her beer.

It was odd to her that she hadn't wanted any of the men she had grown up with to be here with her, but rather she wanted a man she'd only known for a couple of weeks. It spoke of the distrust she had with all the men right now and the fact that she absolutely trusted Nathan with her life.

She took a drink of the beer, her thoughts on what she'd just agreed to. She'd never lived with a man before. Jim had never lived with her. He'd always spent the evening with her and then had gone back to his apartment in town. She should be feeling nervous about this new experience, but she had a feeling Nathan would be a very easy man to live with.

She finished the beer, checked to make sure both of her doors were double-locked and then she went into her bedroom to get ready for bed.

As she changed into her nightgown, another huge sense of relief swept through her. With Nathan here, she would feel safe and secure. She wouldn't have to be so frightened of the dark. Hopefully her fear of the swamp in the dark would pass with each day that went by.

She slept well that night and got up early the next morning. She was surprised by the sweet anticipation that filled her at the thought that Nathan would be there at noon.

One of the first things they would have to do was go to the grocery store. She didn't keep food for two and her cooler was fairly empty. She hoped Nathan wouldn't mind, but if he wanted to eat, then the trip was necessary.

She had no idea what her friends would think about this arrangement. Her women friends would probably just be glad that she had somebody to be with her and keep her safe. She had a feeling that Louis, Jacques and Beau would have a much bigger problem with it.

They would probably be angry and upset that she hadn't depended on one of them. But she just couldn't right now. Somebody had left that note and the voodoo doll for her and unfortunately those men were all at the top of her suspect list.

She spent the morning getting things ready for Nathan. She cleaned and made sure she had fresh sheets for the sofa. She had to go into town to do laundry at the local Laundromat, but thankfully she had done that recently enough that she had plenty of clean bedding for him.

She also made space in her closet for his things. It was all a new experience for her, thinking about sharing her space with a man full-time. She cleared out a drawer in her dresser and then cleaned off a shelf in the bathroom closet so he could put his toiletries there.

It's all only temporary, she reminded herself. Nothing had changed about his timeline for leaving Crystal Cove. He had a life to get back to in New Orleans, and that day would be here far too soon.

But she didn't want to dwell on that right now. All she cared about was he wanted to be her hero and for now she was going to let him. In truth, she needed a hero right now.

Surely with a little time away from the terror in the swamp, she would be okay going out on her own again after dark. At least the monster, if it had been the Swamp Soul Stealer, obviously hadn't found her shanty and she was definitely grateful for that. However, she didn't believe the Swamp Soul Stealer had left her the voodoo doll and the note, and whoever that person was, he definitely knew where she lived. But she didn't want to think about that right now.

The morning flew by and at precisely noon his footsteps sounded on her bridge outside. She opened the door and smiled at him. His camera case was slung around his neck and each of his hands held a medium-sized duffel bag.

"Permission to come aboard," he said with a boyish grin.

"Permission granted," she replied and opened the door wider to allow him and his bags entry. He walked past her and she smelled the delicious scent of him. It smelled like safety.

He set the bags down and took off the camera and placed it on the sofa. "Haven't changed your mind about all this, have you?" he asked.

"No, and I can see by your bags that you haven't changed your mind, either."

"Speaking of bags, where do you want me to put these things?" he asked. His eyes held a sparkle that warmed her from the top of her head to the very tips of her toes.

"I made room for your hanging clothes in my closet and cleared a drawer for you in the dresser. There's also an empty shelf for your toiletries in the bathroom closet."

"You obviously went to a lot of trouble," he replied with a frown. "You do realize I could have just lived out of my bags."

"Nonsense and it was no problem at all. Why don't you get unpacked and settled in and then we need to make a trip to the grocery store. I don't usually keep enough food for two."

"Sounds like a plan," he replied agreeably. He carried both his bags into her bedroom and she sat on the edge of the bed and they talked while he unpacked.

The setting was intimate. It had been years since she'd had a man in her bedroom for anything. At least her nightstands were neat and clean and her bed was made up with the bright pink spread that she loved. There were also several white and pink decorative pillows tossed on there as well.

Still, as he hung his clothes and then tucked things into the drawer she'd had ready for him, it was far too easy to imagine him on the bed with her and between her sheets. The desire she had for this man was completely insane.

Thankfully, it didn't take him long and once he'd stowed his toiletries in the bathroom, they headed out for the grocery store. The fresh air outside cooled the crazy thoughts that had momentarily flowed through her head about him being in her bed.

"Is there anything in particular you're hungry for?" she asked. She was seated in the passenger seat as he had insisted he would drive.

"No, nothing in particular, but we'll share the cooking duties so you aren't always cooking for me," he replied.

She cast him a grin of amusement. "Can you cook?"

"I love food so much I had to learn to cook, so the short answer is yes. I can definitely make a mean burger."

"Then I look forward to having one," she replied.

They continued to talk about cooking until they arrived at the grocery store. Once inside, he grabbed one of the carts and she walked beside him while they shopped.

She had been on a bit of a sexual burn since they'd

been together in her bedroom and her desire for him only increased as they shopped and laughed together.

He looked so handsome in a pair of black slacks and a gray short-sleeved button-up shirt. His hair had grown out a bit and the slightly shaggy style only emphasized his strong features and beautiful blue eyes.

They were in the produce department, playfully arguing about a bag of shredded lettuce versus a whole head of lettuce when she realized she wanted him in her bed. Maybe not tonight or tomorrow night. But before he left town, she wanted to make love with Nathan Merrick.

She suddenly recognized that she'd invited a different kind of danger into her home. She was afraid of physical harm outside and she now had to worry about heartbreak on the inside.

It took them about an hour in the grocery store to get everything they would need for several days. Their time together was off to a great start with plenty of laughter. He'd tried to pay for the groceries but she'd insisted she pay half, so he told her she could work a day for free instead. She finally agreed to that.

He'd been surprised she had agreed to his offer to stay with her. He knew her to be a strong, independent woman, but it was obvious her experience being chased through the swamp had truly shaken her up.

Hell, it had shaken him up when she'd told him about it. He couldn't even imagine the terror she must have experienced. He was just happy that she'd agreed to allow him to stay with her. He wanted to keep her safe for as long as he was here in Crystal Cove. He didn't even want to think about what could happen when he left. Hopefully by that time the Swamp Soul Stealer would be behind bars and everyone could breathe a big sigh of relief.

They got back to her place and between the two of them, carried all the groceries inside in one trip. Once in the shanty, they placed the bags on the kitchen table and then he handed each item to her and she put it away.

It was such a mundane task and yet he thoroughly enjoyed it. As they worked, they talked about all the meals they could make with what they had bought.

"Don't forget, we can always fish for our dinner," she said. Today she looked like another ray of sunshine in jeans and a bright yellow T-shirt. Her smiles were bright and her eyes sparkled. The tears from the night before appeared gone and he was grateful she seemed back to her normal, cheerful self.

"It's nice to know that if all the grocery stores around the world shut down, you could still feed me fish," he replied teasingly.

"You don't fish?" she asked.

"I've never been fishing in my life," he admitted.

"Then we definitely need to remedy that." She picked up several cans of vegetables and stored them in a cabinet. "You have to learn to fish so you can feed me."

"I wouldn't mind learning to fish so I can support you in the manner to which you've become accustomed," he replied.

"Now that's what I'm talking about," she replied with a laugh.

They finished putting all the groceries away and then he looked at her expectantly. "What do you normally do in the afternoons when we aren't out in the swamp working?"

"I usually just chill. I enjoy reading and I always have a couple of library books on hand."

"Hmm, that explains it," he said.

She looked at him curiously. "That explains what?"

"The fact that you're so intelligent."

She laughed, that musical sound that he loved to hear. "I don't know about how intelligent I am, but part of it is due to my mother who homeschooled me. She had me study a wide variety of subjects and she was a tough taskmaster. There were plenty of days I would have much rather been out running in the swamp, but study time always came first."

"Good for your mother," he replied. "Still, reading definitely makes people smarter and wiser. And now I'll just go sit on the sofa and stay out of your way."

He sank down on one side of the sofa, noticing on the other end was a pillow and a folded sheet and blanket. His bedding for the night.

Her bed had looked damn inviting when he'd been in her bedroom, but that wasn't part of their deal. He would be a gentleman and sleep on the sofa…unless she invited him into the bedroom.

Before any steamy visions of that happening could fill his head, he picked up his camera. He always had photos to edit and decide which picture would go best with what text for the book. He certainly couldn't forget the reason he was here.

As he got to work, Angel grabbed a book off the bookshelf and sank down in the chair facing him. The next couple of hours were peaceful, although he found himself gazing at her again and again. Her presence wasn't very conducive to him getting his work done.

Still, with the lapping of the water outside and Angel's presence inside, there was a peace in his heart, the peace that at least for the moment all was right in the world.

It was about four thirty when she closed the book and stood. She stretched by bending first one way and then the other. He tried not to look at her smooth skin that was exposed where the T-shirt she wore pulled up with her stretching. "Are you hungry?" she asked.

"Definitely getting there," he replied and began to put his camera away. "I didn't eat any lunch today."

"I didn't, either."

"How about I fry up a couple of those burgers I told you about? The buns we bought are fresh today and it won't take me long."

"That sounds great," she replied. "And this way I can see if your burgers are really all that."

"Be prepared to be amazed." He finished putting his camera away and then stood.

Minutes later he stood at the kitchen counter ready to make his hamburger patties. He'd bought the specific spices he needed and he now mixed them altogether with the hamburger in a bowl.

She sat at the table watching him and laughed as he tried to hide his spices from her view. She had gotten out the cooktop for him and he had a skillet and a saucepan for a can of baked beans they had bought.

"I'm not used to somebody cooking dinner for me," she said as he began to form the meat into patties and placed each one into the skillet.

"I'm not used to cooking dinner for somebody," he replied. He grabbed the can opener and opened the can of beans, then dumped them into the saucepan to warm. He then turned and grinned at her. "I'm not used to it, but I could definitely get used to it."

"Me, too," she replied with a laugh. Oh, her eyes sparkled so brightly and despite the rising smell of cooking hamburger, he could still smell the alluring scent of her. It had been a constant all afternoon and it drew him to her like a bee to honey.

Twenty minutes later they sat at the table to eat. Besides the hamburgers and beans, they also had potato chips to round out the meal.

"Okay, it's the moment of truth," he said as she picked up the burger. He watched intently as she took her first bite. She chewed and swallowed and then quickly chased it down with a big drink of water. She then gazed at him soberly.

"You don't like it," he said in dismay. "Maybe I put in too much seasoning, or maybe I didn't use quite enough."

She grinned at him then, an impish grin that immediately shot through to his heart. "Actually, it's very good and I love it."

"Woman, you're going to age me long before my time," he said. "So, is it the best burger you've ever had?"

"I do love the Big D's burgers, but I have to admit this one tops theirs hands down."

"And that's exactly what I wanted to hear," he replied.

Their lighthearted banter continued as they ate. Once they were finished eating, she helped him with the cleanup and then they moved back into the living room where they both sank down on the sofa.

As darkness began to fall, she lit the lanterns in the room, giving it all a cozy glow. "I'd say the first day of this experiment has gone very well," she said.

He raised a brow at her. "You consider this an experiment?"

"In a way, yes. I've never lived with a man before, so this is all new to me."

"You didn't live together with the boyfriend who broke your heart?" he asked.

"No, he always lived in town and I lived here. In fact, he never spent the night here. So, I don't know how to live with a man in the house."

"At least you think today went well."

She cast him a soft smile. "You're just an easy man to be around."

"Thanks, I feel the same way about you." She looked so lovely in the lantern light. The glow emphasized her high cheekbones and illuminated her olive skin tone. Her eyes shone like those of a wild animal in the jungle and his blood heated up inside him.

They continued to talk as the night deepened and the sound of throaty bullfrogs came from outside. It was about nine o'clock when she stood up from the sofa.

"I think it's my bedtime," she said. He got up from the sofa as well.

"What are the plans for tomorrow?"

"What do you think about having your first fishing lesson early in the morning?"

"Can you make sure I don't slip in the water and get eaten by an alligator?" he asked.

"I'll make sure you don't get eaten," she replied. "After we do a little fishing, then we can do our usual thing exploring the swamp so you can get more of the photos you need."

"Do you feel comfortable doing that?" He took a step closer to her.

"During the daylight and with you, I feel very comfortable. Besides, if it really was the Swamp Soul Stealer, then as far as I know, he's only taken people after dark."

She took a step closer to him. "So, I guess I'll just say good-night now." Still, she didn't make a move to leave the room or step back from him.

"Would you like a good-night kiss?" he asked, his body heating up once again.

She smiled at him impishly. "How did you know?"

He took another step toward her and then gathered her into his arms. He intended the kiss to be short and sweet, but as always, the moment his lips took hers, he was lost in her.

Their tongues swirled together in a dance of hot desire. Her arms tightened around his neck as she leaned into him. Did he want to make love to her in that moment? Absolutely, and he had a feeling she would have let him…even encouraged him to do so.

But he was also aware that her fear still might be weighing heavy in her heart and she might make a decision tonight that she would regret in the morning when she was thinking more clearly.

With this thought in mind, he reluctantly broke the kiss and stepped back from her. "Good night, Angel."

She looked at him for a long moment and then slowly nodded. "Good night, Nathan." She turned and headed into her bedroom. He heard the door close and then he made up his bed on the sofa and stretched out.

As the fire of his desire for her slowly ebbed away, he released a deep sigh. Living here with her was going to be much harder than he'd anticipated. His desire for her was a living, breathing animal inside him and he knew she felt the same way about him.

Surely that's all it was with Angel. It had nothing to do with love or anything like that. He loved her company. He loved her laughter. He loved so many things about her, but that didn't mean he was actually in love with her.

He didn't want to be in love with her. While he would miss her when he left here, he refused to walk away from here with a broken heart.

He knew the bitter taste of a broken heart. He remembered the absolute searing pain and he never wanted to experience that again. He would be leaving here soon, so as much as he desired Angel, he would never allow himself to fall in love with her.

Chapter Nine

She would have slept with him last night. Angel awakened the next morning with that single thought playing in her mind. She'd wanted to take him by the hand, bring him into her bedroom and make sweet, fiery love with him.

As he'd kissed her, she'd tasted his desire for her and knew he wanted her, too. However, before anything more could happen, he'd broken the kiss and stepped back from her, allowing the moment between them to pass. She now rolled over on her back and released a deep sigh. She should probably be grateful he'd broken up the moment.

It was very early in the morning. The sun wasn't even beginning to peek over the horizon and so she remained in bed and gave her thoughts free rein.

During the years after she and her ex had broken up, there had been plenty of men who had asked her out. She'd rejected each and every offer. After the pain and betrayal of Jim, she hadn't wanted to open her heart up to any man. She had her friends and that had been enough for her.

Until Nathan.

Either he had changed her or she'd grown from the past heartache because she'd opened her heart up to him completely. How foolish was she to pin her heart to a man who was unavailable for a real, lasting relationship.

It wouldn't be long before she'd rouse him to go fishing with her. She knew it would be fun to teach him and they'd have a great time together, as they usually did. Then they'd once again go exploring in the swamp so he could continue to take the pictures he needed.

Once he had the last of the photos he wanted, then he'd be leaving. He would take her heart with him. As much as she'd fought against it, she realized now she was completely and madly in love with Nathan Merrick.

She loved him far more than she'd ever loved Jim. Her love for Nathan was different than it had been with Jim. It was deeper and richer. But in the end, it couldn't…wouldn't last.

Yes, she had been an utter fool. When she'd felt herself falling for him so deeply, she should have stopped being his guide and never seen him again. She should have protected her heart more carefully, but she hadn't and now it was too late. She'd just have to deal with her emotions after he left.

Releasing another deep sigh, she got out of bed. Quietly she crept across the hallway and into the bathroom. She washed her face and brushed her hair, then captured the long tresses into a big silver barrette at the nape of her neck.

Once that was done, she returned to her bedroom to dress for the day. She pulled on a pair of jeans and then a plain light pink T-shirt.

By that time the sun had peeked up over the horizon and it was time to wake up Nathan. If they were going to catch fish, early morning was the very best time.

She walked into the living room, surprised to find him sitting on the edge of the sofa. The lanterns in the room were still burning and in the lamp's illumination he looked sexy as hell.

He wore only a pair of black boxers and his hair was slightly mussed. His bare shoulders were wide and his chest showed muscles she hadn't even known he possessed. Almost instantly a rush of heat infused her.

"Good morning," he said with a smile.

"Good morning to you." She looked at him with a frown. "I didn't expect you to be awake yet. Did you not sleep well?"

"On the contrary, I slept so well that I woke up a few minutes ago feeling refreshed and ready to catch some fish," he replied.

"Then while you get dressed, I'll get the poles ready to go," she replied. She needed him to get dressed as soon as possible, before she snatched him up off the sofa and pulled him into her bedroom.

"Great," he replied. As he stood, she quickly turned and headed for the back door.

Once outside, she drew in a deep breath of the air that didn't smell like Nathan. She gathered the fishing items, which were two poles and a tackle box. She then went to a small tank filled with dirt that contained the earthworms she used as bait. She grabbed a handful of them and then placed them in a small plastic container to take with them.

Once she had everything together, she carried it all into the living room and placed it by the front door. Nathan was obviously in her bedroom getting dressed.

She started to sit on the sofa, but at that moment he came out. Dressed in a pair of jeans and a gray T-shirt, he also brought with him a big grin.

"I've been thinking about this fishing thing," he said.

"And?"

"And I think I'm going to kick your butt by catching way more fish than you do."

"Ha! Is that a challenge I smell in the air?" she replied.

"I believe it is," he said. "How about loser has to cook dinner tonight."

"You're on, loser." With a grin, she handed him the poles to carry while she grabbed the tackle box and worms. Together they stepped out into the golden light of dawn.

"I assume we're going to your favorite fishing spot," he said as he followed behind her across her bridge.

"That's exactly where we're going," she replied.

"You do realize that gives you a slight advantage over me."

She laughed. "Are you already regretting your challenge to me?"

"Not a chance," he replied. "Even though you might have a personal relationship with all the fish in your favorite fishing spot, I'm still going to catch more than you."

She laughed once again. "Time will tell."

It took them fifteen minutes to reach the place where

she usually fished from the bank. She opened her tackle box, removed the lid from the container of worms and then took one of the poles from him.

"Okay, first you need to bait your hook." She took one of the wiggly worms and got it on the hook.

He watched her and then did the same thing with his. "This is going to be a piece of cake," he said once he was finished.

She grinned at him. "And this is how you cast out into the water." She showed him how to throw the baited hook and line into the water.

He raised the pole over his head and then threw his line out. It landed in the water about three feet in front of the bank.

"Uh, you might want to try that again," she suggested, trying not to laugh. "The farther out you are in the water, the better the odds of getting a fish on the line."

"I know. That was just my practice shot," he replied. He reeled the line in and then threw it back out, this time getting it out far enough.

"Now we wait for a bite." She sank down to the ground and he did the same, sitting far too close to her for her peace of mind.

As they waited, they small-talked about what kinds of photos he still needed to get. As he told her what he needed, she realized there weren't that many left. And once he had those, he'd be gone.

He was the first one to jump up as the tip of his pole bent. "Set the hook," she said. "Give it a quick jerk and then reel it in as fast as you can."

He did as she said and reeled in a nice-sized catfish. He crowed with his success and did a silly dance. "Who's the boss now, baby?"

She laughed at his antics. "Our deal wasn't who caught the first fish, it's who catches the most fish." She got up and helped him get the fish off the hook and then showed him how to place it on a stringer. He then rebaited his hook and cast it out in the water once again.

"Sunrise is beautiful here," he observed.

"I love it at this time of the day when the first rays of the sun shimmers golden on the water and birds sing their morning songs from the trees."

"I know living in the swamp is hard, but there is a lot to be said for it," he said thoughtfully.

"I agree that it can be difficult, but there's a much slower pace here than I imagine there is anywhere else. We work hard but we also relax hard. I find such peace here. Of course, I don't know anything different than this."

He smiled, but before he could say anything else, the tip of his pole dipped again with another bite and he jumped back up to his feet.

They fished for about another hour or so and by that time she had caught four and he had two. "Ready to head back?" she asked.

"I hate to go home as a loser, but I admit you beat me fair and square this morning," he replied.

"I can almost smell the scent of dinner cooking," she said with a small grin.

"Oh, so you're a bad winner and will be crowing about your success all afternoon long," he said as they put their equipment away.

"Are you a bad loser and going to pout all day?" she returned.

He laughed. "I don't think I've ever pouted a day in my life."

"Then I like that about you," she replied.

They walked a few minutes in silence. "Maybe we need to go into town and buy a few board games to help pass the afternoons," he said.

"Board games? Like what do you have in mind?" she asked.

"Have you ever played chess before?"

"Yes, I have. My dad taught me years ago and we would often play together. He has a board and the pieces. I'm sure we could borrow it from him. It's time for me to check in with them, anyway. I'll bring them some of the fish we caught this morning and you could meet them."

"I'd love to meet them. Why don't we put off our usual trek through the swamp for today."

"Would you be okay with that?"

"I'm fine with it," he replied.

She could imagine introducing her parents to the man she loved, the man she was going to marry and build a life with, but instead she would introduce him as the biologist friend she'd been working for.

It didn't take them long to get back to the shanty where she put two of the biggest catfish on a stringer to take to her parents and tossed the other four into her floating cage. Then they left to head to her parents' place.

"I'd prefer we not say anything about you staying

with me," she said as they walked. "I don't want to outright lie to them, but I haven't mentioned anything about what's going on in my life right now because I don't want them to worry about me."

"Got it," he replied. "I have to admit, I'm ridiculously nervous to meet your parents," he added.

She flashed a quick backward glance at him. "Why?"

"Because they have to be awesome people to have created a woman like you."

"There you go again, Mr. Merrick, turning my head with all your flattery and charm."

"I'm serious, Angel. You are an amazing woman."

Then love me and stay here with me forever, her heart cried out. But she knew the whole idea of him staying and living in the swamp with her for the rest of his life was ridiculous.

He was a biologist, not a fisherman. He was a teacher and a respected person in his community. Besides, despite all the flattery she got from him, in spite of the fact that there was a wild sexual chemistry between them, he certainly hadn't indicated that he was in love with her.

Maybe it was a good thing he'd stopped kissing her last night and they hadn't gone to her bedroom. She was so confused about what she wanted in her life right now.

Did she want to throw all caution to the wind and make love with Nathan? Did she want to act on the crazy sexual desire she felt for him? She knew without doubt if she gave him an open invitation into her bed, he would take it.

Did she want to carry that memory with her when

he was gone? Or did she not want to have that memory at all to taunt and torment her when he left?

NATHAN THOROUGHLY ENJOYED meeting Angel's parents, who seemed like wonderfully kind and good people. It was obvious they adored their only child and he could easily see where Angel got both her confidence and sense of loyalty and compassion.

It was also obvious her parents still adored one another. It was in their tone of voice when they spoke to each other and in the way they looked at each other.

It made him envious. He wanted that in his own life. He wanted a woman to grow old with and continue to love through the years. He wanted to grow a family with a special woman who he knew would make an amazing mother.

They visited for about half an hour and then left her mother and father the fish Angel had caught and walked out with a box that held the chessboard and pieces inside.

"I'm now looking forward to a challenging game of chess," he said as he followed her home. "I couldn't beat you at fishing this morning, but I'm pretty sure I'll kick your butt at chess."

"Ha, pretty full of yourself, aren't you?" she replied with a laugh.

"Nah, just warning you about what's going to happen."

"The first thing I want to do when we get back is take a nice, refreshing shower," she said.

The day was unusually humid and just walking had

him sweating more than a little bit. "I wouldn't mind taking one myself," he replied.

Instantly his mind filled with visions of them showering together. He would be able to slide the bar of soap across her breasts and down her belly, then he'd pull her close against him as the water played on their heads. He snapped the very hot vision out of his brain before it could go any further.

"I'll let you shower first since you have dinner duty and then I'll shower."

"Works for me," he agreed. So, there would be no shower for two.

They were silent for the rest of the walk. Once they got back to her place, she set the chess game on the coffee table and grinned at him. "I hope you're prepared to get *your* butt handed to you when we play chess."

"Ha, that's not going to happen." He loved it when she grinned at him so teasingly. "I let you beat me at fishing this morning, but I'm not going to let you beat me at chess."

"Oh, you *let* me beat you at fishing? You're a funny man. And now I'll just go grab you a towel for your shower.

She went into the bathroom and returned with a large bath towel. She handed it to him and then gestured for him to follow her outside.

He was surprised by the structure she had built for showering. It was a small wooden enclosure with a large bucket overhead and plastic tubing leading to a showerhead.

"I imagine this looks fairly primitive to you, but it works," she replied.

"Actually, I find it quite brilliant," he replied.

"Thanks. There's soap in the dish and a bottle of shampoo on the floor inside there and all you have to do is open the plastic tubing clip to get the water to run."

"Got it," he replied.

Five minutes later he stood beneath the spray of water. The soap was fresh-scented and he worked quickly, not knowing how much liquid was in the bucket. The water was a bit cool and completely refreshing.

When he was finished, he squeezed the clip to stop the water flow and then dried off. He wrapped the towel around himself and then stepped back into the house.

Angel was seated on the sofa and setting up the chessboard. "Mind if I duck into your room for my clothes."

"Nathan, feel free to go into my room anytime you need anything of yours," she replied. "And while you're dressing, I'll go take my own shower."

He went into the bathroom first and grabbed his deodorant. He then went into her bedroom and took out a clean pair of jeans and a light blue polo. Within minutes he was dressed and then went back into the bathroom.

As he put away his deodorant and spritzed on some of his cologne, he tried to keep all thoughts of Angel taking her shower out of his head. Just imagining it was something he didn't need.

He went into the living room and sank down on the sofa in front of the chessboard. He hadn't realized until now that the board, along with the pieces, appeared to be hand-carved from wood. They were positively stunning.

The water outside stopped and a few minutes later she stepped back inside. A big red towel was wrapped around her body, but the sexy vision of her made him momentarily tongue-tied.

"I'll be out in just a few minutes," she said and then disappeared into the bedroom.

He released a deep shuddery sigh. He wanted her so badly it hurt inside him. Being around her and not touching her was an exquisite form of torture. He didn't love her, but he definitely wanted her far more than he could ever remember wanting a woman before.

She came back into the living room a few minutes later clad in a red-and-white housedress. It was fitted at the top and then swung out from her waist and hips. It looked cool and relaxing and she smelled of the alluring scent that he loved. Every muscle in his body tensed with his desire for her.

"So, are you ready?" She gestured toward the chessboard. "I think we have time for a couple of games before you have to cook dinner."

"I'm ready," he replied and picked up one of the pieces. "Do you know who made this set? These look hand-carved."

"They are. My father made it. He likes to whittle a little in his spare time." She went into the kitchen and grabbed one of the chairs at the table.

"He's very talented," he replied.

She set the chair opposite to where he sat on the sofa

and straightened the chessboard between them. "It's just something he enjoys doing." She sat in the chair. She cast him one of her impish smiles. "I'm so confident I'll even let you make the first move."

"Okay, then."

She was smart as a whip and knew the game well. He had to really concentrate on the moves he was making and that was difficult with her beautiful presence seated right across from him.

They played three games. He won two and she won one. By that time, he needed to start dinner. They both moved into the kitchen where she sat at the table and he opened the cooler to see what he could prepare.

"What do you think about smothered hamburger patties and mashed potatoes?" he asked.

"Sounds good to me. At least I can help you by peeling the potatoes." She got up and pulled the bag of potatoes out of the lower cabinet.

"Okay, then while you do that, I'll put together some awesome patties." He took the pound of hamburger out of the cooler and then grabbed a bowl to put it all together in.

As he gathered up breadcrumbs and various spices, she began to peel the potatoes. Once again, he thought about how nice it was to be working together in the kitchen. It felt natural and right and he wanted this kind of relationship in his life.

Of course it wouldn't be with Angel. It couldn't be with her, but when he got back home, he intended to open himself up fully to the dating game. It was time. He now realized he was ready for a wife, somebody who would fill his days with laughter and conversation like Angel had these last couple weeks.

He also wanted a woman who filled his heart with healthy lust, a lust they could explore every night of his life. He wanted a woman who would rival the lust he felt toward the woman who was now peeling the potatoes.

As they worked, they talked more about her parents. "How did they meet?" he asked.

"Their parents were good friends and often got together to visit. They're the same age and Dad always says when they were both thirteen, he knew he wanted to marry Mom."

"Is that the way lots of relationships form here? With parents being friends?" he asked, curious.

"It's definitely one way that young people meet. But a lot of them just meet when they are going about their lives in the swamp."

Once the potatoes were boiling and the patties were cooking, she sat back down while he manned the burners.

Their conversation moved on to the chess games they had played. "You do realize I let you win the first one so your male pride wouldn't be hurt," she said with a teasing lilt to her voice.

"You're a funny woman," he replied with a laugh. "Actually, I let you win the second game so you wouldn't pout if I beat you in all three games."

"Ha, and you're a funny man," she replied. "And I'm definitely not a pouter."

"And I like that about you," he said, throwing her words back at her. He went to the cabinet of canned goods and pulled out two cans of brown gravy he had bought from the store. He drained the grease off the patties into a coffee can she kept specifically for that purpose and then added the gravy to the patties. He turned down the heat beneath it and covered the pan with a lid.

He then turned his attention to the potatoes. It didn't take long after that to get the meal on the table. They lightly bantered with each other as they ate and then they cleaned the kitchen together.

Once that was done, they settled back into the living room for a couple more games of chess before bedtime. Once again, he found her to be very distracting.

Her green eyes appeared to glow as her gaze went from him to the chessboard. Her scent made it difficult for him to concentrate and her long silky hair begged his fingers to tangle in it while he kissed her until they were both mindless.

He also found her natural intelligence hot as hell, and he was on a slow burn the entire time they played. As darkness descended, she lit the lanterns that were positioned around the room, the soft glow loving her beautiful features.

By the time they decided to call it a night, they were tied. She'd won the first game and he'd won the second. He stood and began putting the pieces back in the box where they belonged while she returned her chair to the kitchen.

"First thing in the morning I'm going to take the pirogue out and do a fish run," she said. "You don't have to come with me. I'll be perfectly safe out on the water."

He frowned. "Are you sure?"

"I'm positive. I don't even have to step a foot on the shore so I'll be completely safe. Besides, the pirogue is a one-person boat."

"And I'm not a fan of dangling in the water and holding onto the side of a little boat," he replied. "As long as you're sure you'll be safe, that's all I care about."

"And I appreciate that. Now, I think I'll call it a night because I like to do the fish runs early," she said. Like last night, she didn't make a move to leave the room. In fact, she took a step toward him. "Do I get a good-night kiss from you?" she asked.

"Absolutely," he replied, even knowing it was going to be sheer torture for him to kiss her and then let her go.

He stepped toward her and she met him halfway. He didn't intend to take her into his arms, but when she wrapped her arms around his neck, he couldn't help himself.

He pulled her shapely body tightly against him and took her mouth with his. She immediately opened her mouth and danced her tongue with his. Hot flames of desire whipped up inside him, creating an inferno.

She was on fire, too. He could tell by how hungrily she kissed him and how she moved her hips against his. He was already aroused, and with her hips rubbing against him, it only intensified.

He finally broke the kiss and stepped back from her. She reached out and took his hand in hers. Her eyes blazed with a deep emerald fire. "Come into my bedroom, Nathan. Come with me and make love to me."

He stared at her for several long moments, looking

for any hint of hesitation or regret from her. He saw none. All he saw was open fiery hunger.

She tugged on his hand. "Nathan, make love to me," she whispered urgently. "You know it's what we both want."

With that, he allowed her to lead him into the bedroom, his heart pounding wildly in his chest. He knew on some level this was all wrong, but his want for her in this moment was far greater than anything else.

Chapter Ten

Angel knew she might regret this in the morning, but it felt like she'd wanted Nathan since the moment she first met him when he was sitting on the side of the trail and looked up at her with his dazzling blue eyes.

The fire inside her burned hot and bright and she wasn't going to deny herself this pleasure any longer. And she knew without doubt it would be a pleasure. Once they were in her bedroom, she lit a lantern, creating a soft glow around the bed.

Then she turned and reached out for him once again. He gathered her back into his arms and his mouth took hers, and at the same time his hands slid from the middle of her back and down across her buttocks. He pulled her even closer to him, close enough that she could feel his arousal and she was quickly lost in him.

His familiar scent stirred her and the feel of his body so close to hers caused her blood to heat to liquid fire as it rushed through her veins.

She didn't know how long they kissed as time didn't matter. They were hungry kisses…fiery ones that only increased her incredible desire for him. Her nipples were erect beneath her housedress and it wasn't long before she wanted more.

She plucked at the bottom of his shirt and he took the cue, stepping back from her so that he could remove his shirt. The lantern's glow played on his muscled chest and she moved close to him once again so she could stroke her hands down his warm bare flesh.

His eyes burned with a brightness she'd never seen before and she wanted to fall into the blue depths and stay there forever. His gaze made love to her long before he'd even touched her body.

She rained kisses across his chest and then stepped back and swept her housedress off and tossed it next to the bed. She was now clad only in a wispy pair of red panties.

"Oh, Angel, you are so beautiful," he said, his voice deeper than usual as his gaze swept down the length of her.

"So are you," she replied. She slid into her sheets while he took off his shoes and socks and then kicked off his jeans, leaving him clad only in a pair of navy boxers.

His body was magnificent. His shoulders were broad and his waist was slim. His legs were firmly muscled and athletic-looking and the sight of him nearly naked stirred everything inside her.

He joined her in the bed and once again pulled her into his arms and captured her mouth with his. His half-naked body against her own felt incredible.

She loved his skin. It was so smooth and warm and tasted slightly of salt. He rolled her over on her back and then slid his hands down her neck and across her collarbone. She held her breath in sweet anticipation and then he touched her breasts.

His hands cupped them for a moment and then his fingers rolled and toyed with her erect nipples. They hardened even more and ached in sweet torment beneath his touch.

She'd dreamed of him touching her like this and in reality it was so much better than she could have ever imagined. His lips slid down the path of his hands, nibbling along her collarbone and then capturing one of her nipples in his hot mouth.

Electrical currents shot off inside her, running from her nipples to the very core of her. Her body was moist and ready for him and when one of his hands slid downward from her breasts, she opened her legs to him.

But he continued to torment and tease her, running his fingers back and forth across her lower abdomen and then her hips, but not touching her where she wanted…where she needed him to touch her the most. At the same time his lips once again plied hers with heated kisses.

She clung to him, her fingers biting into his shoulders as she opened her legs even wider. She gasped as his fingers finally touched her intimately at her core. They danced against her slowly at first. It was a new source of pleasure and sweet torment.

He began to move his fingers faster and faster in a dance that beckoned a rising tension inside her. Higher and higher she flew on a wave of such heightened desire it stole her breath away.

And then she was there, spiraling completely out of control and shaking with the force of her climax. For a moment afterward she was utterly boneless and unable to move, but once that moment passed, she began to caress his chest.

As she slid her hands down his muscles, she followed it with nipping, teasing kisses. She licked and kissed his nipples and then worked her way down his body, down his flat abdomen and then took his hard erection into one of her hands.

He tangled his fingers in her hair and moaned her name as she slid her hand up and down his velvety hardness. He only allowed her to caress him for a moment or two and then he pushed her away and positioned himself between her thighs.

"Yes," she hissed softly as he slowly entered her. He eased halfway in and then paused, as if afraid he might rush her in some way. She grabbed him by his buttocks and raised her legs around him, plunging him deeper and more fully inside her.

He moaned deep in his throat and the sound of his pleasure only increased her own. He moved his hips, slow at first with long strokes in and out of her. Her desire spiraled upward again as he increased his pace.

Their gasping filled the air, along with plenty of moans. She clung to his shoulders as he drove into her faster and faster. Then she was there, once again flying over the moon and then crashing down to earth with her orgasm. She shuddered against him and at the same time he climaxed, groaning her name over and over again.

When it was all finished, he rolled over on his back next to her and for a few moments they remained still, just trying to catch their ragged breaths.

"That was…" he began.

"Explosive," she replied.

"Amazing," he added.

"Incredible."

"Earth-shattering."

She laughed, filled with a joy she'd never felt before.

"Don't tell me it was funny. That would definitely destroy my male ego."

"Oh, it wasn't funny… We're funny," she replied.

He raised up on one elbow and gazed down at her. "We are funny, but you know what isn't? We went into this without any birth control."

"Don't worry, I'm on the pill and I can assure you I'm clean. I haven't been with anyone for a very long time," she replied.

"It's been years since I've been with anyone." He bent down and kissed her softly on the cheek. "Thank you for sharing yourself with me."

"I thank you for the same," she replied. "I've wanted you for a long time, Nathan."

"You couldn't have wanted me as much as I've wanted you," he replied. "Angel, you have been a beautiful torment for me. Every time we touched, I wanted to pull you down and make love with you."

"I have felt the same way," she replied.

"And now, I think I need to get up." He slid out of the bed and grabbed his clothing from the floor.

"Nathan, if you want, you can come back in here to sleep tonight."

He smiled. "I would love to do that," he replied and then left her room. As he went into the bathroom, she stared up at the ceiling where the lantern's light flickered and danced.

Making love with him had probably been a huge mistake and she'd just compounded it by inviting him to share her bed for the rest of the night.

At this current moment she didn't care about anything. Her body still tingled with the feel of his touch and she couldn't think of anything better than falling asleep in his arms.

It would be a memory she would cherish long after he was gone. But she also didn't want to dwell on him leaving right now or how big of a fool she had been in falling in love with the man.

Right now her plan was to enjoy each and every moment of the time she had left with him. She could entertain all her regrets, and there would be plenty, when he was gone from here forever.

When he came back into the room, she rolled out of the bed and headed for the bathroom. Once there she cleaned up and then pulled on the nightgown that hung from a hook on the back of the door.

When she went into the bedroom again, Nathan was already back in the bed. He looked like he belonged there and her heart squeezed tight. She slid into the bed next to him and he immediately drew her close to him, spooning around her with his big strong body.

He rose up and kissed her on her cheek. "Good night, my sweet Angel," he whispered in her ear.

"Good night, my sweet Nathan," she replied softly. She closed her eyes, happier than she'd been in years.

She knew the moment he fell asleep, but she remained awake for a little while just reveling in the sound of his soft rhythmic breathing and in the embrace of his arm around her waist and his body around her back.

She must have fallen asleep because the next thing she knew it was just before dawn. At some point during the night, they had physically separated so thankfully she could ease out of the bed without awakening him.

And thankfully the lantern was still burning so she was able to grab some clothes without fumbling around in the dark. She looked at Nathan one last time. Even in sleep, he was so handsome and looked like he belonged in her bed. He was probably sleeping far better there than on the sofa.

She left the room and went into the bathroom to wash her face, brush her teeth and hair and then dress. Once she was ready, she left the bathroom and headed to the backdoor.

It took her only minutes to be out on the water, using the push pole to guide her to her fishing lines. The sun was just peeking over the horizon, as always painting the swamp in a golden glow.

The real glow this morning was deep in her heart. Making love with Nathan had been beyond wonderful and it had been magical falling asleep in his arms the night before. She had felt a peace, a security she'd never felt before. He had completed her life in ways she'd never expected.

Would he miss her when he was gone from here… from her? When he returned to his life in New Orleans, would he even think about the woman from the swamp who had entertained him for a month?

Now that they'd explored their lust for each other, would his interest in her wane? Certainly that wasn't the case for her. She still wanted him, and her love for him had only grown with their physical intimacy.

Dammit. How had she allowed this to happen? How had she fallen in love with a man who was completely unavailable to have a life with her? Why couldn't she have fallen in love with one of the three men who had been by her side since they were kids? Things would have been so much easier that way.

She shoved all these thoughts aside, determined to just enjoy the beauty and peace of sunrise on the water in the swamp she loved.

This would give her strength when Nathan was gone. She'd always have the swamp to sustain her. She didn't need a man to complete her. She was more than enough on her own.

She still had her parents and her women friends. Eventually she might find a man to love…to marry. However she still suspected that one of her men friends had been behind the voodoo doll and the note.

What she wasn't sure of was if it had been the Swamp Soul Stealer who had chased her through the night or if it had been one of the three men who professed to care about her. If it had been one of them, then why hadn't they come to her shanty? Had the person merely wanted to terrorize her so she'd turn to them for help and protection?

With these troubling thoughts starting to bubble up in her mind, she was grateful to reach her fish lines and gather the fish she had caught. As she got them all up, she baited the hooks once again and then started toward home.

There was a peace in the swamp this morning, but somewhere a monster crept and Angel didn't know if there was just one monster or another one who had her in his sights.

NATHAN AWAKENED AS Angel was leaving to do her fish run. He remained in bed for several minutes, thinking of the night they had shared.

She'd been an amazing lover. She'd been so passionate and she'd driven him half mad with her hot kisses and fevered strokes against his bare skin. She'd met his intense desire with her own and that had been incredibly hot.

Even though he'd been completely sated last night, he wanted to repeat making love with her as soon as possible. His desire to have her again was as fevered this morning as it had been the day before. He'd never experienced this kind of heightened desire for any woman before. What made it even hotter was how much he liked her.

He finally got out of bed and got washed and dressed for the day. He went into the living room and sank down on the sofa to await her return. The shanty felt lonely without her. It was crazy that he felt lonely when she wasn't with him.

His gaze landed on the voodoo doll in the bookcase and he got up to get the doll. Next to the doll was a folded piece of paper and out of curiosity he opened it.

STAY AWAY FROM THE SCIENCE MAN!

The words screamed from the page in bold red ink. He stared at it in stunned surprise. When had Angel received this? And why hadn't she told him about it?

He left the doll on her bookcase and carried the note back to the sofa. He laid it out on the coffee table and stared at it. He believed there had been no secrets between him and Angel. She'd shown him the voodoo doll, so why hadn't she shown him this note, which definitely had the feel of a threat to it?

A touch of anger rose up inside him. He was angry at whoever had left the note for her and almost as equally angry at Angel for not telling him about it.

So who had written it and was it possible that person had terrified her by chasing her through the swamp? The first name that jumped into his mind was Beau. There was no doubt in Nathan's mind that the man was in love with Angel, no matter what Angel felt on the matter. That meant Beau had to have seen Nathan as a threat.

He ruminated on the mystery of the voodoo doll and the note-writer until the sound of the back door opening and closing pulled him from his thoughts.

"Good morning," she said cheerfully as she walked

in. Even though it was early morning, as always, she looked amazing. She wore jeans and a fitted light blue T-shirt.

"Not so much," he replied.

She frowned. "Did you not sleep well?" She stepped closer to him and her gaze fell on the note.

"When did you receive this?" he asked.

Her shoulders stiffened. "What are you doing? Sneaking around in my stuff?"

"Don't deflect, Angel. I hardly had to sneak around to find this," he replied. "So, when did you get this and why didn't you tell me about it right away?"

She sank down on the opposite side of the sofa from him and stared down at the note. "I got it about a week ago and I didn't tell you because I was afraid you'd immediately fire me from my job working for you."

"I probably would have," he admitted. "This definitely seems like a threat, Angel. I would never forgive myself if something happened to you because of me."

"I wasn't about to allow an anonymous note left on my door dictate what I do and don't do," she replied with a stubborn lift of her chin.

"Still, you should have told me about this. I should have known about it."

"Yes, I probably should have told you," she finally admitted. "But to be honest, Nathan, I was enjoying our time together and I didn't want it to end."

Her words, coupled with the look of misery that crossed her features, made any anger he'd felt toward her melt away. "Come here," he said and gestured her into his arms.

He held her for a long moment and then released her. "So, who do you think wrote it?" he asked.

She shrugged. "I don't know, but I think it has to be one of the men I thought I could trust with my life."

"My first suspect would be Beau. No matter what you think, Angel, I believe the man is in love with you and would see me as a threat. He wouldn't want you hanging around me. He wouldn't know that we're not in love with each other and that when I leave here, he'll still have an opportunity to woo you."

"I don't have any romantic feelings toward any of those men, and I never will. To me, this is more the style of Jacques or Louis. They are far more hotheaded than Beau," she replied.

"Looking back on that night when you were chased through the swamp, is it possible it was one of those men and it wasn't the Swamp Soul Stealer?" he asked.

A line danced across the center of her forehead as she frowned. "Yes, I suppose that's possible. The only thing that made me believe otherwise was the fact that the person didn't come to my home. All the men know where I live, so if it was one of them chasing me, then why didn't they just show up here?"

"Maybe it was just an attempt to scare you so you'd turn to them for comfort and safety," he suggested. "Maybe whoever it was believed that they would be here with you instead of me."

"Maybe. I'd thought about that, but instead I turned to the one man I trust in all this and that is you." She released a deep sigh. "I don't want to talk about all this anymore. Why don't we head out so you can get more of your pictures?"

"I've got to say this, Angel, you are one strong, independent woman. Most women who received a note like that would have stopped seeing me immediately."

She offered him a small smile. "You should know by now that I am not most women." She got up from the sofa and he did as well. "So, do you forgive me for not telling you?"

He couldn't help but smile back at her. "You're forgiven, but I don't want you to keep anything else like this from me, deal?"

"Deal," she replied.

Aside from his physical lust for her, he also had a lot of admiration for her. "Then let's go get some photos." He picked up his camera from where it rested at the side of the sofa.

He double-checked that he had his stun gun in his pocket and then they took off. In truth he now had almost all the photos he needed, but he was reluctant to tell her goodbye.

He couldn't leave now while she was so vulnerable. If it had been one of her male friends who had chased her through the swamp, then it had been an evil thing to do. If one of those men had romantic feelings for her, then why hadn't they just spoken to her about them?

They stayed out in the swamp until almost dinnertime with him taking mostly unnecessary photos. She fried up a pan of catfish for dinner and afterward they played a couple games of chess.

"I think it's a wise idea for you and I to go into town

in the morning and talk to the chief of police," he said when they had finished their last game and he was putting the pieces away in the box.

She looked at him in surprise. "Why? I'm sure there's nothing he can do about any of this."

"I think he should at least know about what's been going on with you," he said. "Angel, I think it's really important. So can we go into town tomorrow?"

She sighed and stood from the chair where she had been sitting for the chess games. "Okay. If you really think it's necessary, then how about we plan on going around nine in the morning?"

"That sounds fine." He stood as she pulled the kitchen chair back to where it belonged.

She came back into the living room. "I guess I'll just say good-night, then." She didn't wait around for a kiss but instead turned to head into her bedroom.

"Good night, Angel."

She flashed a quick smile over her shoulder. "Good night, Nathan." She then disappeared into her bedroom and closed the door behind her.

Nathan made out his bed on the sofa, sorry that he wasn't sharing hers. Aside from the delicious pleasure of making love to her, he'd loved having her warm sweet-smelling body to spoon around. The cuddle afterward had been almost as good as the sex.

Tonight it would just be him and the bullfrogs and the gentle lap of the water. It was a far cry from the sound of car horns honking and sirens blaring that he was accustomed to being jarred by when he was trying to fall asleep in New Orleans.

It was odd, but the noise of the swamp had begun to sound like home. But, of course, that was impossible. This wasn't his home and it never would be. Still, once he left here, he would retain the sounds of the swamp at night and the memory of a beautiful woman to lull him to sleep.

THE NEXT MORNING at nine o'clock they were in his car and headed into town. She held both the voodoo doll and the note in her lap and she was very quiet.

"Are you nervous?" he finally asked.

"No, not exactly nervous, but I do hate to bother Etienne with all this," she replied.

"I still think he should know about it. If I'd known about the note, I would have encouraged you to talk to him immediately after you received it."

She released a deep sigh and fell silent once again. It was impossible for him to know what was going on in her mind. He knew how difficult this all had been for her and he wished he had the words to make it all go away.

But he didn't and so he didn't try to find any words and instead allowed her to have her silence. The police station was in a fairly large one-story building. It was painted turquoise and had two large plateglass windows in the front.

He parked and together they got out of the car and he ushered her into a lobby. There were half a dozen chairs in front of the windows and a reception window, which a uniformed officer stood behind.

He opened a window in the glass front of his area.

"Hey, folks." He greeted them with a friendly smile. "What can I do for you two this morning?"

"We'd like to speak to Chief Savoie," Nathan said.

"Can I just get your names?"

Nathan told them who they were. "Okay, just have a seat and I'll see if he's available right now," the officer replied. He closed the window and left the desk through a back doorway.

Nathan and Angel sat side by side in the gray plastic chairs in front of the windows. She clutched the voodoo doll and note close to her chest with one hand and he reached out to hold her other hand.

She not only allowed him to but she also squeezed his hand tightly, as if needing his support in this moment. "You know there's nothing to be nervous about," he said softly. "You're the innocent victim here."

"Like I said before, I'm not exactly nervous. It's just that showing all this to Etienne makes it all so real."

"It is real, honey, and that's why we need to be here."

At that moment the officer returned to the front window. "If you two want to go through the doorway on the right, I'll take you back to the chief."

They followed him into a long hallway and he stopped at the second door on the right. He knocked on the door and then opened it. "Chief, they're right here." He then opened the door wider to allow the two of them inside.

Nathan had never met the chief of police before. He was younger than Nathan had expected. His dark slightly curly hair looked like it was weeks past a haircut, but his gray eyes appeared sharp with intelligence.

He rose from his desk as they entered the room and he held out a hand to Nathan. "I know Angel, but I don't believe we've met before," he said.

"I'm Nathan Merrick," Nathan replied as he gave the chief's hand a firm shake.

"Nice to meet you, Mr. Merrick. Please, have a seat," he said and gestured toward the two chairs that were directly in front of his desk. Once they were all settled, Chief Savoie smiled at them. "Now, what can I do for you both this morning?"

"There's probably nothing you can do to help the situation I find myself in, but Nathan insisted it was important for me to speak to you about it," Angel said.

"Okay, so tell me what's been going on," Chief Savoie replied.

Angel began telling him, starting from when she had found the voodoo doll on her door. She handed him the doll and he examined it carefully and then set it aside on his desk.

She then showed him the note and once again he looked at it closely and set it next to the voodoo doll. Finally she told him about being chased through the swamp. As she recounted the horrifying event, her voice rose slightly in pitch and tears filled her eyes. Once again Nathan reached for her hand and held it tight.

"Well, it's obvious you didn't heed the note's warning, because the two of you are here together now," Etienne said.

"You know me, Etienne, I don't take well to people telling me what to do," Angel replied.

"Actually, I've moved in with Angel for her protection but I'm only going to be in town for a short while so I'm hoping this somehow gets resolved quickly."

The chief frowned. "The first thing we need to do is get your fingerprints so they can be excluded when we dust this note." He looked at Angel. "Is there anyone you've been having problems with? Have you had words with anyone?"

Angel shook her head. "No, nobody."

"Do you have any suspects in mind?"

She hesitated a long moment and then nodded. "Louis Mignot, Beau Gustave and Jacques Augustin and maybe Mac Singleton from the grocery store." The names fell from her lips as if released from under an enormous pressure.

Etienne wrote down the names and then looked back up at her. "And why do you suspect these men in particular?"

She explained her reasons, specifically the fact that they were the only four men consistently in her life. "Mac has always given me the impression he has a small crush on me and as for the others, I've just lost all trust in any of them because somebody left me those things and they're the only men in my life."

"Is it possible a woman left these for you?" Etienne asked and turned his attention to Nathan. "Has any woman expressed an interest in you since you've been in town? Maybe somebody who would be jealous of your time with Angel?"

"No, there's been nobody," Nathan replied firmly. "However, I do believe Beau is in love with Angel, and he would certainly see me as a threat and wouldn't want Angel having anything to do with me," Nathan added.

"I'll bring them all in for questioning," Etienne said.

"I didn't want to add to your workload," Angel replied miserably. "I know you have your hands full with the Swamp Soul Stealer."

"Speaking of that, I think that you can rule him out as the one who chased you through the swamp," Etienne said.

Angel frowned. "Why?"

"You said the man who chased you roared loudly several times with rage. In all the instances of the disappearances of people, on the nights they were taken, not a single sound was heard. And believe me, my men asked dozens of people if they heard anything. Our belief is he sneaks up on his victims silently."

Angel stared at him for a long moment. "So, then it was probably one of the men I mentioned to you. He is either a person I call my good friend or a man I've done business with for years."

"Unless the Swamp Soul Stealer has changed his ways, which I highly doubt, then yes it was probably one of the men closest to you. Angel, I swear I'm going to do everything I can to get to the bottom of this."

"We would appreciate it," Nathan said. "Unfortunately I'll be leaving Crystal Cover in a matter of weeks and when I leave here, I want to know that Angel is safe."

"The thing that concerns me is there is a definite escalation at play," Etienne said. "First the doll, then the note and then the chase through the swamp." A deep frown cut across his forehead. "My concern for you is what happens now? If the escalation continues, then what is this person's next move?"

Angel's hand grew cold in Nathan's as Etienne's question hung heavy in the air. What, indeed, might happen next?

Chapter Eleven

A wave of depression swept through Angel as they walked out of the police station. Her discouragement had begun the day before when Nathan had told her that Beau couldn't know she and Nathan weren't in love with each other.

It had been a stark reality check that he could so easily say he wasn't in love with her. She wasn't sure what exactly she'd hoped for, but she'd definitely hoped for a little more from him considering all they had shared.

Now to compound things, she had to face the fact that one of her "friends" may have left her the note and the voodoo doll. One of those "friends" may have chased her through the swamp roaring like a wild animal and scaring her half to death. What kind of a friend did something like that to a vulnerable woman he supposedly cared about?

She cast a look at the man in the car's driver seat. As if he sensed her gaze, he turned and offered her a small smile. "Are you okay?" he asked, his soft voice like a caress against her ear.

"I will be," she replied.

"There's no doubt in my mind that you will be," he

replied. "I can imagine all the thoughts and emotions that are flying around inside your head after speaking to the chief."

That's only the half of it, she thought. Thank God at this point she hadn't spoken to him of her love for him, even though it had and still shouted loudly in her head.

She released a sigh and stared out the passenger window. It was time for her to start distancing herself from Nathan. Although she wasn't fool enough to kick him out of her home. She still needed his safety and protection and if she looked deep within herself, she still wanted to enjoy his company until the final day when he left here.

But there would be no more hot kisses between them, no more tumbles into her bed. She had to start protecting herself from the crazy love he had evoked in her.

"Are you ready to head out for more picture-taking?" she asked as he parked the car.

"Do you really feel like doing that today?" he asked.

"Why not? We've taken care of the police business of the day, so we might as well get to your work now."

"Okay, then I'm all in," he agreed.

They got out of the car and once they were at her shanty, he grabbed his camera and they took off. As usual, his camera stayed busy as they went first up one trail and then another.

They talked a little bit, but she just really wasn't in the mood to chat about inane things. The reality that one of her friends, one of the men she had known since childhood had possibly chased her through the swamp suddenly hit her hard.

As they continued their trek through the trails, she recognized Nathan was working hard to put her in a better mood and she forced herself to try to get there.

Surprisingly, by the time they knocked off for the day around four o'clock, she was in a better frame of mind. She still had a big, strong man staying with her and Etienne had promised to do some investigating into the matter. Besides, she'd never been one to entertain a foul mood for very long.

When they got back to the shanty, they each took a shower and then she started on dinner preparations. They decided to keep it simple. She fried up some fish and made a box of mac and cheese.

"Want to play some chess after we eat?" he asked when the two of them were at the table.

"Sure, I wouldn't mind beating you a few more games before bedtime," she replied.

"Ha, you're always crowing before but you'll be crying afterward," he replied with those teasing eyes of his.

"We'll see who is crying afterward," she replied with mock confidence.

This was part of what she enjoyed—their easy banter and playful competition with each other. That continued through their meal, and once the cleanup was complete, they moved into the living room and set up the chess game.

They had just started playing when a knock fell on the door. "Hey, Angel," Beau's voice cried out.

A sudden tension gripped her as she got up to answer. It was all three of the men... Louis, Beau and Jacques. "Hi," she said and opened the door to allow them all in. They brought with them what felt like an angry energy and Nathan immediately stood up from the sofa.

"Well, doesn't this look like fun," Jacques said as he gazed at the chessboard. "Angel, apparently, you're a woman of many hidden talents. I didn't know you could play chess, and I definitely never suspected you of throwing your friends under the bus."

The tension inside her increased. "Why don't you all have a seat," she said, uncomfortable with them all standing and glaring at her.

Beau took the chair she had been sitting in to play chess. Louis stalked into the kitchen to grab a chair and brought it in and sat, while Jacques threw himself on the opposite end of the sofa from Nathan. She sank down in the chair where she usually sat when they all came over.

Finally they were all seated, but their obvious displeasure with her still stood tall in the room. "Why in the hell would you even bring up our names to Etienne? Do you really think that any one of us is responsible for that voodoo doll or note?" Louis asked, his dark eyes searching her features.

"I'll be perfectly honest," she replied. "Aside from the note and the doll, a few nights ago somebody also chased me through the swamp and terrified me."

Beau sat back in his chair, appearing surprised by this news. "I hadn't heard about you being chased. Are you sure it wasn't the Swamp Soul Stealer?"

"According to what Etienne told me this morning, it's doubtful," she replied.

"And you believe it was one of us?" Jacques asked. He shot a narrowed gaze at Nathan. "Have you considered that it might have been him? Looks like it got him a pretty cozy setup here."

She stared at Jacques and she couldn't help the burst of laughter that escaped her at the very idea of Nathan being the one who had chased her in the darkness through the swamp.

She sobered quickly. "There's no way it was Nathan. The man who chased me knew the swamp very well."

"Personally, I was shocked when I got word that the chief of police wanted to interview me," Louis said. "I figured he wanted to talk to me about gator poaching, but when he asked me about my relationship with you, I was very surprised that you had put my name in his mouth."

Angel released a deep sigh. "I'm sorry, my intention wasn't to hurt any of you, but somebody is doing these things to me and I don't know who and I don't know why. I went to Etienne because I'm afraid, and I have Nathan here with me for the same reason. I... I don't know who to trust anymore."

Beau released a string of curses. "I can't believe what I'm hearing. Angel, I can't believe you don't know that you can trust me with your very life. I would never ever do anything to harm you."

"I wouldn't, either," Jacques added.

"I agree," Louis said. "Angel, you're barking up the wrong tree by suspecting any of us."

"But you have to understand the position I'm in," she replied. Angel was grateful that the anger the men had brought in with them seemed to have dissipated some. "Etienne asked me what men were in my life and so I told him. The three of you weren't the only names I gave him."

"It's time for us to go," Jacques said abruptly and rose from the sofa. He looked at the other two men. "We've told her how we feel and there's nothing more to say here."

Beau and Louis moved the chairs back into the kitchen and then the three of them walked to the door. Angel got up from her chair and opened the door for them.

"Good night Angel... Nathan," Jacques said and then the three of them left.

Angel locked the door behind them and then returned to the easy chair opposite the sofa. She released a deep sigh. "I don't know why but I didn't expect that."

"I certainly didn't expect it so soon," Nathan replied. "Chief Savoie must be taking this quite seriously and I'm glad for that."

Angel wrapped her arms around herself as a chill suffused her. "I just didn't think this through. I'm almost sorry I gave Etienne their names."

"Angel, you had to tell Etienne their names," Nathan said in protest. "This isn't a game, honey. Somebody is terrorizing you."

"Did you get any feeling about them? Did one of them appear guilty to you?" She searched his features, wishing he held the answer for her.

He shook his head. "I watched each one of them closely and unfortunately as far as I'm concerned it could be any one of the three. One of them is a very good liar."

"Unless it's Mac from the grocery store."

He frowned at her. "Do you really believe Mac is the guilty party?"

She released a deep sigh. "Not really. In my heart of hearts, I believe it's one of the men who just left here. What worries me is now whoever it is knows Etienne is investigating and I'm really afraid about what's going to happen next."

HE STEPPED INTO his shanty and roared as a new rage nearly drove him to his knees. The bitch. He'd warned her to stay away from the science man and now she'd moved the bastard in with her.

He'd been watching her…watching them. He'd seen the day Nathan moved his duffel bags into her house and then he'd never left.

Slamming his fist into the back of his recliner, he thought about the two of them in bed together. The visions of them making love made him absolutely sick. That photographer was getting what was rightfully his.

She was a disloyal bitch and Nathan Merrick was an interloper who didn't belong here. However, he couldn't really blame Nathan for becoming besotted with Angel. She'd probably seduced him with her dark green eyes and perfect body. The poor city boy hadn't stood a chance against the very hot swamp woman.

It was Angel he blamed, and it was Angel who would pay. She was the one who had forgotten where she came from and she was the one who had forgotten she belonged to him.

He'd continue to watch and wait for the perfect opportunity. Sooner or later she would have to pay and this time it would be with her life. Only with her death would he finally be free of her.

For the next four days Angel and Nathan fell back into an easy routine. In the early mornings she took her pirogue out to do her fish runs and when she returned, they ate breakfast and then took off into the swamp.

Nathan continued to take more photos he didn't really need. He'd pretty much gotten everything he needed for his book and then some. However he still wasn't ready to leave without things being more settled for Angel.

Like her, he worried about what escalation would look like. There had been no more visits from the men, but Nathan was relatively sure one of them was the guilty party. He just didn't know which one and he didn't know what might happen next for Angel.

There was no way he could just bail on her now. He cared far too deeply about her to leave right away. He was hoping Chief Savoie would find the answer and get the guilty man behind bars in a relatively short period of time.

Tonight they were planning on her making a fish run into town and this time he would be by her side. He now looked across the room where she was curled up in her chair reading a book.

She really was the most beautiful woman he'd ever

met. There was no question he was going to miss her a lot when he left. There had been no more lovemaking between them, no kisses or any other kind of physical touching since the night they last made love.

His desire for her hadn't waned at all, but she'd made it clear nothing was going to happen between them again. Each night she told him a quick good-night and then just as quickly went to her room and closed the door behind her.

There had been a hundred times over the past few days that he'd wanted to touch a strand of her long hair and tuck it behind her ear, kiss the cheek he'd expose and then run his lips across to capture hers with his. But instead he'd given her space because that's obviously what she wanted.

Still, one of the things he was going to miss about her was the deep friendship they had built. She'd been not only a good friend, but also a confidante in the time he'd spent here with her.

He had shared all kinds of things with her about his personal life and about his past. She'd shared with him as well. He felt like she knew him better than any woman had ever known him before.

She finally closed her book and got up from the chair. "We'll eat a quick dinner before we go since the fish run usually takes about two hours or so."

"Sounds good to me." He put his camera away while she went into the kitchen.

Hot dogs and chips were on the menu for that night and it was about four o'clock when they sat down to eat. "I love a good hot dog," he said.

She laughed. "You love a good anything if it's fit to be eaten."

"This is true," he replied with a grin.

"We'll need to make another trip into the grocery store tomorrow. It's time to restock the cooler."

"We can do that," he replied. "And maybe it's time we stop in at the ice-cream place again."

"That would be nice," she replied and smiled.

Her smiles—he was definitely going to miss those when he left here. They were so bright and beautiful. "Then we have a plan, a fish run tonight and then ice cream tomorrow night."

"I like that plan."

She ate two hot dogs and he ate three. The dinner cleanup was a breeze and by that time it was after five o'clock. He helped her get her fish together to take into town. It was a big job and took them two trips from her back deck to the cooler in her truck. She went back into the shanty to light some of the lanterns for when they returned after dark.

"I can't believe you do this all by yourself on a regular basis," he said when they were ready to leave.

"I'm used to it," she replied. "It's my work…my life." She got into the driver's side of the truck and he got into the passenger's side.

It was a cloudy gray evening providing a false early twilight. "Looks like we might get some rain," he said.

"That wouldn't be a bad thing," she replied. "I always like it to fill up my rainwater barrels."

"I would think the humidity would help with that."

"It helps, but a little rain never hurts things. Besides,

I love the way the air smells after a good rain. Why? Are you going to melt?" she asked teasingly.

"Not at all, in fact I like to dance in the rain. Maybe we can have a jig or two later."

She laughed. "You are a bit of a goofball, Nathan, but I like that about you."

"And I think you have a little goofball in you, and I like that about you, too." He released a small sigh. It was moments like these that he would miss with her.

She was exactly the kind of woman he wanted to find to fill his days and nights. When he got back to New Orleans, that's who he'd be looking for, a woman just like Angel.

"So, where do we go first?" he asked as they entered the small town.

"The grocery store."

He heard a faint rise of tension in her voice. "Are you nervous to see Mac?"

"Maybe a little. I'm not afraid of him, but I'm sure it's going to be more than a bit awkward if Etienne has already interviewed him."

"Will it affect your business dealings with the store?" Nathan asked curiously.

"I don't think so. Mac has always been a professional when it comes to business. At least I'm hoping that doesn't change. The store pretty much depends on me to keep them stocked in fish and I depend on them to sell my fish to."

"Then hopefully this will all go okay," he replied as she pulled up behind the grocery store at a loading dock. "I need to go inside to get Mac to come out."

"I'll go with you," he replied and together they got out of her truck. He felt tension wafting off her as they went up the loading ramp and in the back door that brought them out next to the meat and fish area.

Mac came out from behind the glass enclosure. He nodded at Nathan and then gazed somberly at Angel. "Chief Savoie had a chat with me this afternoon," he said. "Angel, I hope you know I would never do anything to hurt or scare you."

"Mac, I'm sorry but Etienne asked me about my male friends and associates," Angel replied.

"I had no idea about what's been going on in your life, and I'm so sorry to hear you've had problems, but, Angel, I'm not one of them," he said.

He appeared completely earnest to Nathan. He didn't believe Mac was the guilty party. He still believed it was one of the three men who had come to her house and acted so outraged about being interviewed by Chief Savoie.

"Shall we go look at some fish?" Mac asked.

"Absolutely," Angel replied, relief in her tone.

"Let me go grab Joey and the cooler and we'll meet you outside," Mac said.

"I don't think he's the one," Nathan said as the two of them stepped outside the store.

"I don't, either," she replied. "And thankfully that went far better than I expected."

They had just reached her truck when Mac and a young kid came out carrying a large cooler. Angel got up into the bed of the truck as did Mac and the teenage boy.

Nathan stood next to the back gate and watched with interest as Mac picked from the variety of fish Angel had provided. The whole transaction didn't take long.

As they drove toward the café, the dark clouds overhead had thickened even more, turning the last gasp of day into the darkness of night.

"The stop at the café always takes a little bit longer," Angel said. "Antoinette likes to bicker over prices."

"And I'm sure you aren't a pushover," he observed.

"Ha, not hardly, however I let her believe she's getting one over on me so she walks away happy," she replied.

"And that's what makes you a savvy business woman." Thankfully he could tell the tension that had gripped her before they'd gone into the grocery store was gone. She now appeared completely relaxed and in her element.

She drove up the alley behind the café and once again they got out of the truck. She asked a kid hanging out by the back door to go get Antoinette.

Moments later the older sturdy woman came out with a big guy carrying a cooler. "Nathan, this is Antoinette LeBlanc, the owner of the café. Antoinette, this is my friend, Nathan Merrick."

"He likes my burgers and fries," Antoinette said, surprising him that she even knew what he ate when he was inside the café.

"Nice to meet you and yes, I definitely like your burgers and fries," Nathan replied.

"Now, let's talk fish," she replied. To Nathan's surprise the short round woman easily jumped up into the bed of the truck. She was followed by the man with the cooler and then Angel.

Once again Nathan watched the transaction with interest. This was a large part of Angel's life and if he stayed here, it would become a part of his.

Whoa, where had that thought come from? He wasn't staying here. He had a life in New Orleans to get back to. As much as he had come to love many things about the swamp and the lifestyle here, he certainly wasn't staying.

As the wrangling began between Antoinette and Angel, he admired Angel's skills. The two women went back and forth until finally they both appeared satisfied with the transaction.

"Mission accomplished," he said when they were both back in the truck and headed home.

She flashed him a smile. "It was nice having your support tonight."

"I didn't do anything," he protested.

"But you were here with me, and I just want you to know that I really appreciate it," she replied. "I have to admit, Nathan, I'm really going to miss you when you're gone."

It was the first time she had mentioned his leaving. "I'll miss you, too. I'll miss so many things about this place," he admitted.

"If you remember, I told you once that if you stuck around long enough, you'd fall in love with the swamp," she replied. She pulled into the parking lot and stopped the engine. She unbuckled her seat belt and then instead of getting out she turned to gaze at him.

The lights on the truck were still on, so he could see her lovely features in the illumination from the dashboard. "Nathan," she said as a frown danced across her forehead. "I need you to know that I don't want you to stay here just for my benefit and safety. Once you have all your photos, then I want you to leave just as you'd planned. You aren't responsible for me."

"Trying to get rid of me?" he asked in an effort to lighten the suddenly sober mood.

"Not at all, at least not until you have what you need for your book. I just want you to know that you don't owe me anything when your work is finished here."

"I recognize that, but I still have some more photos to take," he replied. It was a tiny white lie. She didn't have to know he had all the photos he needed. "You're probably just afraid I'll beat you in more chess games."

A small smile erased the line across her forehead. "You are something else, Nathan Merrick." She turned out the truck lights and then they both got out.

"Maybe tomorrow morning I could try to beat you at fishing," he said as they started up the trail with her in the lead.

"You could try to beat me," she replied with a laugh.

When he left here, he would carry the memory of her laughter deep in his heart. It wasn't just the sound of humor, but it was filled with such a vibrancy and a lust for life.

They were about halfway to the shanty when he heard a rustle behind him. He started to turn to see what it was, but before he could, something crashed down on the back of his head.

The tremendous blow sent him straight to the ground, pain screaming through his skull. He gasped for air and tried to fight against the bright stars that swam in his brain.

The last thing he heard before complete darkness descended was a rumble of thunder and Angel's scream.

Chapter Twelve

There was a loud rustle on the trail behind her and Angel turned to see what was going on with Nathan. For a brief moment she was confused as her brain tried to make sense of the scene before her. Nathan was on the ground and not moving. Had he fallen?

Then her gaze focused on the man standing over Nathan. He was clad all in black and wore a ski mask. He held in his hand a short thick leafless branch. She screamed and then turned and ran.

Terror gripped her by the heart, squeezing so tight she could scarcely draw a breath. It wasn't just fear for herself, but for Nathan as well.

Was Nathan dead? Oh, God, if he was, then it was all her fault. He shouldn't have been here with her. She'd known there was danger around her and she'd invited him into the danger. And now he might be gone forever.

Deep sobs escaped her as she continued to race through the darkness and thick foliage. A deep roar resounded from behind her. It was the roar of unbridled rage.

It came from too close behind her. She tried to increase her speed, gasping and fighting to get some distance from the person who chased her.

As she ran, she fumbled at her waist to get her little sister out. She tried to staunch her cries, hoping that she could lose the man and hide from him like she had the last time.

Hopefully then she could circle back and help Nathan, if help was possible for him. Her heart ached for him, but she couldn't help him unless she got away.

She tore through the Spanish moss and tried to push through the vines and limbs that threatened to slow her down. Once again the man bellowed, the frightening, horrendous sound shooting icy chills through her.

Lightning rent the night sky and thunder rumbled overhead, only adding to the madness of the night. Her brain raced with questions. Who was the man chasing her? Was it one of the men she called her friend?

Maybe she should just stop running, turn and confront him. If it truly was one of her friends, then maybe she could talk some sense into him.

But what if it wasn't one of those men? Perhaps she could lose him and run to her shanty for safety. She could hole up there while he continued to hunt the swamp for her. Or maybe she just needed to dive in somewhere and hope she stayed hidden until he moved away from her.

All she knew for sure was he was gaining on her. She had to make a decision about what to do before he caught up with her. Her tears had stopped, unable to be sustained as she raced for her life.

She finally dove into a tangle of vines and thick undergrowth. As she had the last time, she pulled herself into the tightest ball she could make and then she tried to stop breathing so he wouldn't hear her.

It took only moments before he was on the trail near her. The sound of his ragged breathing as he paused nearby only made her fear intensify.

Lightning once again flashed across the sky. *Don't let him see me. Please don't let him find me*, she prayed. She had to survive this so she could help Nathan.

Please let Nathan be okay. Please, please don't let him be dead. She squeezed her eyes tightly closed as hot tears burned there. He didn't deserve any of this. A loud boom of thunder reverberated and once again the man chasing her released a roar to rival nature's sound.

Angel couldn't help the tremors that shot through her body. The leaves around her shook slightly and her pursuer moved closer to her hiding place. With a will-power she didn't know she possessed, she suppressed any more shivers that might give away her hiding place.

Seconds ticked by…long minutes passed with him standing so close to her she thought she could reach out and touch him. Who was it? And what did he want from her?

Thankfully the man moved on down the trail.

A shudder worked through her and she remained hiding for several long minutes. She heard him roar again, but he was far enough away that she felt rela-tively safe and rose from her position. She waited an-other few minutes and then she headed for her shanty. She'd hide out there for a little while to make sure the hunter was really gone and then she'd go to Nathan. He had to be okay. He just had to be.

She crept through the various trails as quietly as possible. She could no longer hear the sounds of her pursuer. As she got closer to her shanty, she began to run. She needed to be inside where hopefully the man chasing her didn't know where she lived. Or, in the case of her friends, the person wouldn't come to her front door.

As she reached her bridge, deep sobs began to escape her once again. She cried because she didn't know if Nathan was dead or alive, and she wept from the sheer terror of the night's chase. Lightning continued to slash the darkness of the skies and it was followed by loud rumbles of thunder.

She finally got inside, and she closed and locked the door after her. She collapsed on her sofa and tried to catch her breath and stop crying. Dammit, who had been after her? And what had he done to Nathan?

The thought of Nathan on the ground and not moving brought new tears to her eyes. Had Nathan been stabbed? Had he been bludgeoned by the thick wooden baton the man had carried? What was Nathan's condition and how much longer should she wait before she went back outside?

A loud boom sounded on her front door, pulling a new scream from the very depths of her. She jumped up from the sofa with her knife held tight in her hands.

Another violent bang on the door sounded. Before she could react, her front window exploded inward. Glass and wood crashed to the ground inside. The man in the ski mask hurtled through the opening and into the room. He waved the big baton-like stick in his hand.

"Who are you?" Angel screamed as she backed up from him. "Who are you and what do you want from me?"

"I want you dead," he yelled. "I'm going to beat your beautiful face in until you no longer exist."

She stared at the masked man in disbelief. She knew that voice. "Louis?"

He took a step toward her and pulled the ski mask up and off his head. He threw it down next to him and then glared at her. In the glow from the lanterns, she saw that his features were twisted with an anger she'd never seen before.

"Louis, what's going on? Why are you doing this?" She took another step back from him. "Why?" She looked at his angry features searchingly.

"You belong to me, Angel. I tried to warn you to stay away from him."

"So, it was you who left me the voodoo doll and the note," she replied as she slid backward another step.

He gave a quick nod. "You were supposed to be mine. You belong to me and yet you invited Nathan into your bed." His dark eyes simmered with his rage.

"What do you mean? I never belonged to you. I belong to nobody," she replied.

"That's not true," he replied angrily. "We talked about getting married. We talked about being together forever. Dammit, Angel, you belong to me."

She continued to stare at him. She searched her brain, trying to remember a time when they'd ever spoken about marriage. She finally remembered. "Louis, I was ten years old when we talked about it," she replied incredulously. "Louis, we were just kids."

"It doesn't matter," he screamed, his features twisted with his anger. "I loved you, but I don't love you anymore. I hate you, Angel. You allowed that man to kiss you, to touch you and now I completely hate you."

"But, Louis, you're my friend," she implored, trying to reach the man who had cared about her, the man she believed would never hurt her.

"You aren't my friend. You're nothing but a nasty slut and sluts need to die." He raised the wooden stick and advanced toward her. He swung at her. She managed to duck and the blow missed her.

When he swung the second time, he struck her on the shoulder. She gasped as the painful blow momentarily stole her breath away. "Louis, please…you hurt me," she managed to gasp.

"Don't you get it, Angel, I want to hurt you. I'm going to enjoy killing you," he replied, and then he bellowed, the sound seeming to rattle the entire structure of her shanty.

Before she could recover from the painful blow to her shoulder, he hit her again. This time the strike hit the back of her hand and knocked her knife to the floor. "Die, you bitch," he yelled.

She began to scream and cry as she now knew Louis meant to kill her. There was no way to reach the man who had been her friend. He was gone, usurped by the monster who stood before her.

Tears blurred her vision as she dove for her knife

and grabbed it. As she quickly turned over on her back, Louis leaped on top of her.

He apparently hadn't realized she had the knife in her hand. She felt it sink deep into his stomach and saw the widening of his eyes. "You bitch," he hissed. He raised the stick, but before he could hit her with it, she twisted the knife in his belly.

His arm fell to the side and with a deep moan, his eyes closed. With deep sobs racking her body, she shoved at him to get him off her.

She managed to push him over and she scooted backward on the floor like a crab as she stared at him. Blood. Oh, God, there was so much of it. It covered the front of her. It covered her hands.

Horror swept through her as she continued to grapple with everything that had just happened. She'd killed her friend, although the man who had been in her shanty... the one who now was dead on the floor, hadn't been the Louis she knew. This man had been a monster, apparently twisted by what he'd believed was love for her.

She wasn't sure how long she sat there when she heard Nathan shouting her name from outside. She jumped to her feet and ran to her door. She quickly unlocked and opened it and threw herself into his arms.

"Thank God you're okay," she cried as he wrapped his arms tightly around her. "I was so scared."

"I'm okay, and thank God you're okay," he replied.

She looked up at him. "It... It was Louis and I stabbed him and I... I think I killed him." Her sobs overwhelmed her as she clung to Nathan and wept into the front of his shirt. "He was going to b-beat me to

death. He…he said I was a slut and I needed to die. I…
I killed him, Nathan."

"Shh, it's okay, Angel. You did what you had to do,"
Nathan replied. "Come into the bedroom. We need to
call Chief Savoie."

On trembling legs, she allowed Nathan to lead her
into the bedroom where she collapsed on the edge of
the bed while he remained standing. "I'll be right back,"
he said.

"Wait…where are you going?" she asked in a panic.

"I just need to check on Louis," he replied. "I want
to see if we should call for an ambulance."

He walked out of the room and she stared after him,
her brain still working to make sense of everything that
had just happened. She couldn't believe that Louis had
hung on to the words she'd spoken as a young girl.

She had said she'd marry Louis when she grew up,
but she'd only been a kid at the time. Around that same
time she'd told Beau and Jacques that she'd marry them,
too.

She looked up at the sound of Nathan coming back
in the room. "No ambulance is necessary. He's gone."

She buried her face in her hands and began to weep
once again as she thought of the man she had stabbed…
the man who had been her close friend since childhood. She'd had no choice but to protect herself but
she mourned deeply for how badly things had gone.

Nathan made the call to get Chief Savoie to the
shanty and then he went back into the bedroom and
sat next to Angel, who was still softly weeping.

He threw his arm around her shoulder and pulled

her tight against him. She leaned into him and slowly began to pull herself together. She drew in deep gulps of air and finally straightened up.

She gazed up at him and her eyes widened. "Oh, Nathan, I haven't even thought to ask you if you're okay." She grabbed his hand and her eyes once again filled with tears. "The last time I saw you, you were on the ground and not moving."

"I'M OKAY," he assured her, although his head still ached. "The bastard hit me over the head from behind and knocked me out cold." He squeezed her hand. "At least I have a hard head, and when I came to, all I could think about was getting to you. Thank God you're okay, Angel. That's all I wanted. I needed you to be okay."

He'd been so afraid for her. When he'd regained consciousness, he'd been so terrified for her safety. He'd heard her screams coming from her shanty and he'd run as fast as he could to get to her.

Thankfully she was alive and even though he'd thought one of the men was the guilty party, it had still been a shock to see Louis sprawled out on her floor.

He couldn't even imagine what was going on in Angel's head right now. Not only were Louis's actions a deep betrayal, but she had also killed the man.

She was quiet and gravely pale as they sat silently side by side on the bed to wait for law enforcement to arrive. He held her hand tightly, knowing that she needed all the support he could give her.

Still, deep in his mind as he sat next to her, he realized it was finally over. She was no longer in danger and he would be free to leave here and go home. But he didn't want to think about that right now. He wouldn't leave until he knew for sure that Angel was going to be okay, both physically and mentally.

"Angel… Nathan," Chief Savoie's voice called out. They both got off the bed and Angel leaned heavily against Nathan as they left the bedroom.

Within minutes there were police officers working the scene and rain had begun to patter on the roof. Chief Savoie grabbed a kitchen chair and carried it into the bedroom and then gestured for Nathan and Angel to follow him there.

Once again the two of them sat on the bed while Chief Savioe sat on the chair facing them with a mini tape recorder in his hand. "First of all, do either of you need any medical attention?"

"I don't," Angel replied.

"And I don't, either," Nathan replied, even though he suspected he suffered from a mild concussion.

"I need to get statements from you both. Do either of you mind if I record this conversation?" the lawman asked.

They both indicated they didn't mind and then Nathan began to give his statement. He started with the fish runs. "Everything went fine and then we started walking back here from the parking lot. We hadn't gone far when I was hit on the head from behind. I was immediately knocked unconscious."

Angel picked it up from there. As Nathan heard what had transpired in the shanty between her and Louis, his blood ran cold. If she hadn't had her knife, there was no doubt in Nathan's mind she would have been killed by Louis.

"It was obviously a case of self-defense," Chief Savoie said when they'd finished. "Unfortunately, Angel, you're going to have to find another place to stay for the night while we finish things up here."

"I'll take her to the motel with me," Nathan replied. "Can we pack an overnight bag?"

"Of course. I'll be in the other room when you're ready to leave." The chief picked up the kitchen chair and left the bedroom, and Nathan got to his feet.

"I could go stay at my parents' place for the night," she said, not moving from the bed.

"Is that what you want to do?" he asked.

She released a deep shuddery sigh. "Not really. I... I don't feel like I'm in the right frame of mind to go to them."

He crouched down in front of her and pushed a strand of her hair behind her ear. "Then come to the motel with me. You can be in whatever frame of mind you need to be in."

Her beautiful green eyes held his gaze. "Are you sure you don't mind? I'd get my own room but I really don't feel like being alone right now."

"Angel, I want you to stay with me." He rose to his feet once again. "Now, let's pack our bags and leave this all to Chief Savoie."

It took them only minutes to get bags together and then they left the bedroom. Angel immediately faced the front door with her back to Louis's body on the floor.

"We're just waiting for the coroner to get here," Chief

Savoie said. "But I have everything I need from you two right now, so you can go ahead and leave."

"We'll be at the motel if you do need us for anything," Nathan replied, then he guided Angel out the door.

The rain had turned to a fine drizzle and they were both quiet as they made their way to his car in the parking lot. He walked close behind her and wondered what she was thinking.

She'd been through a horrible trauma tonight and despite the fact she was a strong woman, something like this would be too much for anyone. It would break anyone.

She remained quiet on the ride to the motel and he didn't attempt to make her talk. He wondered if she was in some sort of daze. If she was, and it was a daze of self-protection, then he was grateful for it. But sooner or later she'd have to process what had gone down tonight.

They reached the motel and Angel sat in the car while he went into the office and got them a room. He returned to the car and drove them down to the room number.

"You go on inside," he said and handed her the room key. "I'll grab the bags."

They both got out of the car and he popped the trunk to retrieve the two bags while she disappeared into the room. A few minutes later he placed the bags on the floor next to one of the beds. He'd gotten a room with two double beds, not knowing what she needed or wanted from him.

She sat on the edge of one bed, looking achingly

vulnerable. Her T-shirt held the violence of the night in blood streaks and her face was still unnaturally pale.

"I need a shower," she said and rose to her feet.

"Are you hungry? Do you want me to get you anything? I could order in or go run to get something."

She shook her head and grabbed her bag. "No, I'm not a bit hungry, but if you are, then feel free to get yourself something." With that, she disappeared into the bathroom.

Nathan sank down on the bed closest to the door. He wasn't hungry, either. His head still ached and now that he knew it was over and Angel was safe, he was exhausted.

The shower spray sounded from the bathroom and he got back up and opened his bag. He hung the shirt he had brought with him and then pulled out his toiletries and a clean pair of boxers. He then turned on the lamp next to his bed and closed the curtain over the front window. Once Angel was finished, he'd jump in the shower.

He remained stretched out on the bed until Angel came into the room. She was dressed in a sleeveless pink nightie. He had no time to dwell on how beautiful she looked for what caught his attention was a huge dark bruise on her shoulder.

He jumped up off the bed and approached her. "Oh, Angel. Is that what Louis did to you?"

"Yes, he hit me there before I could duck away," she replied.

"I wish I could touch it with magical fingers and make it disappear. I wish that somehow I could kiss it and make it all better," he said fervently. It was definitely a nasty bruise.

She smiled. "And I like that about you." The smile immediately disappeared. "It will be okay. It's just going to take some time to heal."

"I would have killed him for you," he said softly. It was true. He would have done whatever was necessary to protect her.

"I know," she replied.

For a long moment they merely gazed at each other. He was grateful to see that some of the color had returned to her face.

She sank down on the edge of the bed closest to the bathroom with her hairbrush in her hand.

"I'm going to pop in for a quick shower," he said. He grabbed the boxers and bag of toiletries and went into the bathroom.

The whole night felt like a nightmare and even though it was over, it wasn't over yet for Angel. He knew without a doubt that she would replay this night in her mind for a while to come. It would be the stuff of nightmares.

He figured he'd stick around for another few days and then it would be time for him to go home. The thought brought him no real happiness but rather it was just something that was going to happen, something that had to happen.

He got out of the shower, pulled on his boxers and then even though he needed to shave, it was far more important that he get back in the room with Angel.

When he came out of the bathroom, she was already

in bed with the sheet pulled up tightly around her. It was obvious she wanted to sleep alone.

"Are you tired?" he asked as he pulled down the blankets on the other bed.

"I'm utterly exhausted."

"So am I," he admitted. He got into bed. "Are you ready for the light to go out?"

"Ready," she replied.

He turned off the lamp, dousing the room into darkness except for where a faint shaft of light danced out of the bathroom. He'd left the light on in there in case either of them got up in the middle of the night.

"Good night, Angel."

"Good night, Nathan," she replied.

The room was quiet, with just the monotonous hum of the air conditioner's fan blowing. He stretched out on his back and stared up at the dark ceiling. All his thoughts were on the woman in the bed next to him.

She had shown very little emotion since it all had ended. Was she really that strong? It was definitely going to take him a while to unwind and actually go to sleep. He wasn't going to easily forget the vision of Louis dead on the floor and Angel covered in his blood.

He didn't know how long it was before she softly called his name. "Nathan, would you mind just coming over here and holding me for a little while?"

"Honey, I can definitely do that." He immediately got out of his bed and slid into hers. He took her into his arms and he could feel the frantic beat of her heart against his.

With the scent of her filling his head and the warm

curves of her body in his arms, this felt right. It felt right that he was here with her in this moment…to comfort her in her hour of need.

She began to cry. They were soft but deep sobs as she clung to him. He didn't ask her any questions or speak to her in any way other than in soft whispers meant to soothe.

She cried for a while and then the sobs slowly stopped. He could feel her utter exhaustion now and knew the best thing for her was to get some sleep.

He spooned himself around her back and then pulled her tight against him with his arm around her waist. He knew the moment she fell asleep once her breathing became deep and rhythmic. It was only then that he allowed himself to fall asleep as well.

Chapter Thirteen

Angel had no idea what time it was when she awakened. The room was dark but she sensed it was way past sunrise. Nathan was in the bed next to her and for several minutes she just listened to the sounds of his deep even breaths.

She was grateful he'd been there for her through the night as she'd tried to process everything that had happened. She'd tried to figure out if she'd had any other option rather than killing Louis. Her brain had worked around difference scenarios but at the end of each one the end result was the same.

The man who had burst into her shanty hadn't been her good friend. There had been nothing of Louis in the monster who had confronted her and she'd had no choice but to protect herself. If she forgot that, she had the aching pain in her shoulder to remind her.

It was going to take time for her to get over everything that had happened. And the one thing she knew for sure was her time with Nathan was at an end.

She'd suspected for the past couple of days Nathan had been taking pictures he didn't need. She knew he'd just been sticking around for her protection. Now she no longer needed his protection. The danger had passed and she was safe.

Tears burned hot at her eyes as she thought about telling him goodbye. It was going to be the most difficult thing she'd ever done in her life.

She had only herself to blame for the pain. She'd allowed herself to fall deeply in love with him. When she'd first started feeling so much for him, she should have stopped things. But instead she had encouraged them, knowing that at the end of it all was heartbreak.

Unable to stay in bed any longer, she quietly got up, grabbed her overnight bag and then went into the bathroom. She washed up, brushed her hair and then put on the jeans and T-shirt she'd brought with her.

She then stepped out of the bathroom. "Good morning," Nathan said and sat up.

"Oh, I hope I didn't wake you," she replied. The sight of him with his hair charmingly mussed from sleep and his bare chest gleaming in the light from the bathroom caused her heart to squeeze tightly.

"No, you didn't wake me," he replied. "How are you doing this morning?" The look he gave her was filled with such caring.

"I'm okay." She sank down on the bed that hadn't been slept in.

"Why don't I get dressed and we go to the café for some breakfast, and while we're there we can check in with Chief Savoie."

She frowned. "Breakfast at the café?"

"Angel, you might as well face it all now. You know

everyone will have heard what happened last night. You need to show people that you're okay."

She sighed, knowing he was probably right. Besides, she wasn't even sure they could return to her place yet, so they might as well get some breakfast.

"Far be it from me to stand between a man and his morning meal," she replied, forcing a lightness to her tone.

He grinned at her. "That's my girl. Give me fifteen minutes or so and I'll be ready to go." He got out of the bed, grabbed the shirt that was hanging and his bag and then disappeared into the bathroom.

She got up and opened the curtains, allowing the morning light to fill the room. A look at her phone let her know that it was just after nine. She couldn't remember ever sleeping so late.

True to his words, about fifteen minutes later Nathan came out of the bathroom. He was dressed in a pair of jeans and a navy button-up, short-sleeved shirt. "Make sure we have all our things out of here and I'll check us out on the way out," he said.

"I have all my things," she said and grabbed her bag.

"Okay, then let's head to the car," he replied.

Minutes later they were checked out of the room and on their way to the café. "Are you hungry?" he asked.

"Maybe a little bit." She was definitely hungry for things she couldn't have. She hungered for his love. She wanted him to stay here with her forever. But each moment she spent with him now only led to their goodbye.

She steeled herself as he pulled up in front of the café and parked. As usual the place was packed and she suspected most of the morning conversations were probably about her and what had happened the night before.

Nathan gripped her elbow firmly as they walked in. She felt the curious gazes that followed them as they took a booth toward the back. Marianne greeted them and immediately pulled Angel to her for a tight hug.

"Girlfriend, I'm so glad you're okay," she said when she finally released Angel. "I can't believe it was Louis. I'm not going to say anything more right now, but, Angel, you know you have your girlfriends to lean on. We're all here for you."

"And I appreciate that," Angel replied and then slid into the booth opposite Nathan. She knew she could count on her friends. But she wasn't sure what to expect from Beau and Jacques. The three men had been thick as thieves. How would they feel about her now? She'd killed their friend. Would they understand that it had been self-defense? That she'd loved Louis until he'd tried to kill her?

Marianne took their orders and minutes later they both had coffee. "How are you doing?" Nathan asked, his gaze soft on her. "I seem to be asking you that a lot."

"I'm okay," she replied and broke eye contact with him. She had to start distancing herself from him. If she gazed at him for too long, she'd start to cry and that was the last thing she wanted to do.

They were halfway through their meal when Beau and Jacques came in and immediately beelined to their booth. Angel steeled herself, not knowing what to expect from them.

"Mind if we sit?" Beau asked. He didn't wait for

an answer as he slid in next to Nathan and Jacques sat next to her. "I'm so glad we found you here. Angel... We didn't know."

"We had no idea it was Louis who was terrorizing you," Jacques said.

"And we understand that you only did what you had to do," Beau said, his dark eyes simmering. "Angel, I would have killed him myself for what he put you through."

Once again tears pressed against her eyelids. She was so very lucky to have friends to support her through all this. She'd been worried about how these two men would react to her, but she realized they cared about her enough to be okay with the choice she'd had to make.

The two stayed only a few minutes more and then left. "Feel better?" Nathan asked.

"Much better," she admitted. "I was so worried about how they would feel about things."

"You have a great support system around you."

"I know, I'm very lucky," she replied. She was a very lucky woman to have survived what she had and to have wonderful friends around her. But in one area of life, she was very unlucky because the man she loved didn't love her back.

ONCE THEY FINISHED up breakfast, Nathan called Chief Savoie, who told him the investigation was complete and they were free to return to the shanty.

As they drove toward the parking place, he shot several glances toward Angel. After the men had left the café, she had grown quiet and distant.

As always, he couldn't begin to guess what was going through her mind. Did she dread returning to her home? Had the peace she'd always had there now been forever tainted by the violence that had occurred there? For her sake, he hoped that wasn't the case.

He wanted to support her however he could, but he wasn't sure what to do for her in this moment. Time... It would just take time for her to heal. He planned on sticking around for another week or two so he could be her support and make sure she was healing.

They reached the parking lot where he stopped the car and took off his seat belt. She made no move to get out. She stared straight ahead for several long moments, then released a sigh and took off her own seat belt.

"Are you dreading this?" he asked.

She turned to look at him and her beautiful eyes simmered with emotion. "A little bit. I just wonder how the police left it." She sighed again. "I've never been nervous about going home before."

He reached out and took her hand in his. What he really wanted to do was wrap her in his arms and hold her until she was okay. "At least you don't have to worry about being in danger anymore."

She squeezed his hand and then withdrew it from his. "Thank God there is that. Okay, let's head in." He grabbed their bags and together they got out of the car.

He followed behind her as they walked through the trails to get to her shanty. The swamp was alive all around them with birdcalls and rustling brush as little animals scurried to go about their morning business.

Her shanty came into view and the first thing he

saw was that the broken window had been boarded up. It was a nice thing for the police to do before they left and it gave him hope for what they'd find inside. Hopefully there were no blood stains left behind for her to clean up.

When they reached the front door, Angel pulled her house key out of her pocket and unlocked the door. He heard the audible breath she took and then she opened the door and they went inside.

It was a bit dark inside with the only light coming from the window in the kitchen. But even in the dim light he could see that thankfully, other than the board on the window, there was no indication that anything had happened here. Chief Savoie and his men were to be commended for the total cleanup that had taken place.

He could feel Angel's relief as she walked around the room. "Are you okay?" he asked.

She stopped walking and turned to face him. "There you go, asking me again. I'm okay. It's all going to be fine." She lit a couple of the lanterns and then sank down in her chair as he sat on the sofa.

"Who do you have to talk to in order to get a new window?" he asked.

"Brett Mayfield. He's a handyman and one of the few people who will come in and do work in the swamp. I'll call him later today," she replied.

"What do you want to do this afternoon? Are you up to going to your fishing spot and doing a little fishing?"

"No." She stared at him for a long moment. "What I am up for is you leaving here today. It's time you pack your bags and go home."

He gazed at her in stunned surprise. He wasn't ready to leave here…to leave her. "Angel, are you sure that's what you want?"

She looked away and nodded her head. "It's what I want. I'm safe now and it's past time for you to go back to your own life." She gazed at him once again. "I need you to go, Nathan. I'm ready to be alone again."

He swore he saw a glint of tears in her eyes that belied what her words were saying to him. "Angel, I… I don't know what to say. My plan was to stay here with you a little while longer."

"Cancel that plan," she said. "Pack your bags and go." She got up from the chair and he rose as well.

There was a bite of anger in her tone, an anger he didn't understand. "Angel, have I done something wrong?"

She released a deep sigh. "No, you've done everything very right, Nathan. You've made me laugh and you've made me think. You've made me feel safe and you've filled up my life in a way I never thought was possible."

The words fell out of her quickly, as if released from under an enormous pressure. But they certainly didn't explain why she was asking him to leave now or the sharpness in her tone.

"In fact," she continued, "you've done everything so right that I've fallen in love with you. I'm in love with you, Nathan, and every moment I spend with you now is sheer torture for me."

Once again he stared at her in stunned surprise. She was in love with him? He hadn't seen this coming and his heart squeezed and tightened his chest.

"I... I don't know what to say," he finally replied.

"Then don't say anything. I thank you for everything you've done for me, but please just pack your bags and go. I'll be out on the back deck."

He watched as she walked through the kitchen area and then disappeared out the back door. She was in love with him? Surely she was mistaking friendship for love. He'd been here with her through the rough times and she was confusing gratitude for love.

He went into the bedroom and began to pack up his things. She might be mistaken about a lot of things, but she'd been very clear she wanted him gone.

His heart ached with a depth of emotion he didn't want to examine right now. All he knew was he hadn't been ready to tell her goodbye yet. He'd just wanted a little more time with her.

It didn't take him long to gather his things. He set his two bags and his camera by the front door and then headed for the back door.

He couldn't leave here without saying goodbye. She'd been such an important part of his life for the past five weeks. He loved her deeply, but he wasn't in love with her. He couldn't be because he had to go back home.

He stepped out on the back deck where she stood at the railing looking out on the water. She turned at the sound of him and her eyes were filled with tears.

His heart squeezed even tighter, making it difficult for him to breathe. God, he hated to see her pain...pain that apparently he was causing her. He'd never meant for this to happen. She'd known from the very beginning he wouldn't be staying here with her.

"Angel... I'm so sorry," he said. "The last thing I ever wanted was to hurt you."

"I know." She swiped a tear off her cheek. "This isn't your problem, Nathan. It's mine. I hope your book is an amazing success."

"Thanks. So, I guess this is goodbye?" Dammit, he didn't want it to be. Even now he wanted to draw her into his arms and hold her body against his. He wanted to feel her heartbeat and smell the scent of her. But, of course, he didn't do that. He knew in this moment she wouldn't want any kind of touch from him.

"Goodbye, Nathan," she said softly and turned her back to him. This was it. It was time for him to leave.

"Goodbye, Angel." There was nothing left to say... nothing left for him to do except abide by her wishes and go. She remained on the deck while he went back into the shanty and grabbed his things.

As he walked down the bridge away from her, he couldn't even begin to sort out all the emotions that rushed through him. It was over. It was done. He had what he needed to finish his book and it was time to go home.

ANGEL SAT AT her favorite fishing place and waited for a bite. It had been a week since Nathan had left and the pain of his absence still ached deep inside her.

She missed the sound of his laughter, so deep and robust. She missed their conversations and that silly little grin of his when he was teasing her. She even missed the click of his camera.

She had a feeling she would never ever again love as deeply, as completely as she'd loved Nathan. He'd left an imprint in her heart that would never go away.

But life went on. The window in her shanty was fixed and she'd fallen back into her usual routine. Her friends had been wonderfully supportive and she told herself she was fine despite the tears that often overwhelmed her at unexpected times.

With the week that had gone by, her tears were coming less frequently now even though the pain of loss still resided deep inside her.

She jumped to her feet as the end of her pole dipped. She jerked to set the hook and then reeled in a nice-sized catfish. As she took it off the hook, she couldn't help but remember the last time she'd been here with Nathan.

They'd had such fun fishing together. He'd made her laugh so hard with his antics and his desire to beat her at catching more fish than her.

She rebaited her hook and then cast it back out in the water and sat once again. At least she had the swamp and she no longer had to worry about it holding a monster who was after her.

The Swamp Soul Stealer still continued to dominate the news but there had been no leads in the cases. Colette Broussard remained in a coma and Angel had heard through the grapevine that Etienne often spent late nights sitting in her hospital room.

"Angel." The deep familiar voice came from behind

her. Was she so lovesick she was imagining Nathan's voice?

She jumped to her feet, whirled around and gasped as she saw him standing in the small clearing. "Nathan," she exclaimed in stunned surprise. Was this some kind of dream? Was he just an imaginary mirage created by the desire in her mind?

"I was hoping I'd find you here," he said and took a step closer to her.

"Nathan, wha…what are you doing here?" Had he forgotten something? Had he left something important at the shanty? She hadn't found anything of his.

It was sheer torture to see him again. He wore jeans and a royal blue shirt that did amazing things to his eyes. Oh, he had such beautiful eyes.

"I went home from here and got settled back into my life and I thought I was going to be just fine, but I haven't been fine. I missed the sounds of the swamp at night and walking leisurely through the trails, but more than anything I missed you, Angel." He took another step closer to her.

"Before I left here, I told myself that I loved the sound of your laughter and the conversations we had. I convinced myself that I loved absolutely everything about you, but I wasn't in love with you. I was wrong, Angel. I was only fooling myself. I'm totally and madly in love with you and I can't imagine my life without you."

He stepped forward and drew her into his arms and her love for him exploded through her heart and soul. He loved her. The words rang through her with happiness. It was all she'd wanted but...how could it possibly work between them?

"I'll tell you something else," he continued before she could say anything. "I have fallen in love with this wild and beautiful place. I want to spend my days here and fall asleep with you in my arms and the sounds of the swamp lulling me to sleep."

"But what about your work?" she asked.

"I realized I could do much of it, including teaching classes, by utilizing the place in town you told me about. I can make my life work for me just fine from here. So, I have a question for you." He pulled her more tightly against him. "Is there room in your shanty for a biologist nerd who loves you with all his heart?"

"Oh, Nathan," she replied breathlessly. "Of course there's room for you."

"So does that mean you're going to marry me and have my babies?"

"Yes...yes, I'll marry you and have your babies." She barely got the words out of her mouth and then his lips were on hers kissing her with a love and caring she could taste.

When the kiss ended, he gazed at her with those beautiful eyes of his. "I'm deeply in love with you, Angel Marchant."

She smiled up at him. "I like that about you, and I'm deeply in love with you, Nathan Merrick."

He laughed, that deep rumble of joy she loved to hear. "And I like that about you."

She frowned up at him. "Are you sure you really

want to do this, Nathan? Are you really ready to leave New Orleans for a life here in the swamp?"

"I'm more than sure. I can easily leave the city behind for the life and love I've found here with you." That boyish grin she loved so much danced to his lips. "And I'm still determined to beat you by catching more fish than you."

She laughed and as he kissed her once again, she knew that her life with him was going to be filled with laughter and fun and love forever more.

Epilogue

Etienne sat in the hospital room where Colette Brous-sard slept in her coma. Machines clicked and whirred in an effort to sustain her life.

He vaguely remembered seeing her around town be-fore she'd been kidnapped. She'd been a pretty woman with her long hair and dark eyes. Now that beauty had been marred by whatever hell she had been through at the hands of her captor.

She'd been malnourished and it had shown in her skinny frame and gaunt face. She'd had three broken ribs and a fractured arm, along with too many bruises to count.

The intravenous feeding tube had managed to put a little weight on her now but she still appeared ill and too thin. The bruises had also begun to heal and her arm had been set in a cast.

Everything that could be done was being done in an effort to help her. Etienne needed her to wake up. He hoped and prayed that she would lead him to the man... the monster dubbed the Swamp Soul Stealer.

The fact that she'd been found alive gave him hope for the others who had been kidnapped. He'd thought they were all dead, but Colette was proof the others might still be alive.

He liked ending his nights here with her. He hoped that in some crazy way his presence might soothe and comfort her, that he might give her the strength to fight through the darkness she was in. He fought the impulse to draw her hand into his.

Her parents had been killed two years ago in an accident with a drunk driver, and Colette had been their only child. So there were no family members vying for time with her. She was alone except for Etienne.

The doctors had told him that one day next week they were going to begin to bring her out of the medically induced coma. Hopefully at that time she would be strong enough to wake up and be able to help him find the monster who had done this to her.

Who had starved her and beaten her to within an inch of her life? Who was the monster who walked the swamp and kidnapped both women and men? She had to wake up and help him find the Swamp Soul Stealer. At this point she was all Etienne had to solve the mystery and get a human monster behind bars.

* * * * *

Look for the next book in
New York Times *bestselling author Carla Cassidy's
miniseries, Marsh Mysteries, coming in May,
only from Harlequin Intrigue!*